CW01091450

AND THE DAYS GROW SHORT

Also by Ted Sherrell:

Kingdom of Cain
The Lonely and the Lost
Milltown
A Bitter Wind from off the Moor
Nor the Years Condemn
Point of Order, Mr Chairman

And the DAYS GROW SHORT

Ted Sherrell

UNITED WRITERS
Cornwall

UNITED WRITERS PUBLICATIONS LTD
Ailsa, Castle Gate, Penzance, Cornwall.

British Library Cataloguing in Publication Data:
A catalogue record for this book is
available from the British Library.

ISBN 1 85200 094 5

Printed in Great Britain by
United Writers Publications Ltd
Cornwall.

To
my dear wife Ann
for her constant help and support over the years.

To
our sons and daughters-in-law:
Neill, James, Matthew, David, Tina and Debbie

and

the next generation:
Thomas, Philippa and Jasmine.

May they ever enjoy the written word.

Chapter One

The June sun beamed down benevolently as George Tennant strolled languidly, and just a little aimlessly, across the wide, imposing square of the old town, a smallish bag of groceries clutched in his left hand. He glanced about him as he angled his walk in the direction of his car parked in front of the ancient Guildhall. It was a lovely place, he mused, and he was glad he lived near it. Yet, despite the loneliness of where he now resided, he was pleased he dwelt in the country. Any town, no matter how small, was still too large for him these days.

He reached his magnificent Jaguar – his pride and joy – milky white and rather ostentatious in the small car park, stored the groceries in the boot, unlocked the driver's door and climbed in. After putting on a Mantovani tape, he clipped on his seat belt, started up the engine and nosed out of the compound.

He moved out into the Square, turned right into Tavistock's main street, then motored steadily along it, and out of town. He was soon in the country, surrounded by the Devon of the picture post-card and holiday brochure. It was the greenness of it all which captivated him, and never failed to do so; and at all times of the year, whatever the weather. It was that more than anything else which had enticed him to come down here to live – though for Janet the attraction had been the leisurely pace of life and the relative peace. For years they had both longed to make London a mere memory, so one day, when life had been decidedly kind to them, they made the decision that the house would go on the market and their new home would be in Devon.

That had been almost four years previously – four years which had often seen fickle fate in malevolent mood.

He turned off the main Okehampton road, then moved along a

high hedged lane with the barren 'last wilderness' that was Dartmoor, looming above him. He passed a few farms and a couple of hamlets before the road became a hill and the first scrub and boulders of the moor appeared on either side. Within a quarter of a mile of reaching the foothills, he had turned off the narrow road onto a newly tarmacadamed drive which angled itself quite steeply up to a fine looking old house gazing unseeingly out across the rolling Devon countryside which lay between itself and Tavistock.

George drove his Jag up the drive and around to the spacious area in front of the house. Alighting, he went to the boot, took from it his purchases, carried them around to the back door of the dwelling, unlocked it and took them into the kitchen. A light lunch in the large garden at the front of the house was called for on such a glorious day, he reasoned. So he cut himself a brace of slices from a loaf which had been in the oven no more than two or three hours earlier, added a pat of butter and a hunk of Stilton to the plate, took a can of beer from the fridge and went out to one of the picnic tables set in the garden.

As he munched his spartan meal and gazed out across rural Devon from his eyrie, he felt unusually at peace with the world. Life, with all its tricks, its loneliness, he mused, was not so bad when viewed from a reasonable height and with the sun shining. He realised after a few minutes, though, that whilst the peace was not being shattered, it was, nonetheless, being disturbed. For in the distance he could hear, distinctly, a female voice shouting out, at intervals of about fifteen seconds, what appeared to be a single word, though what it was he could not tell.

The shouting continued, coming ever closer – and it was not long before he decided that the word being bellowed was 'Bob'. Intrigued by it all, he arose from his picnic table, and walked down to the bottom of the spacious lawn. Reaching the thick but low privet hedge which bounded it, he cast his glance in the general direction from which the staccato call was coming. About three hundred yards to his right on the open moor, he saw a figure on horseback moving slowly in his direction – and shouting at the top of her rather melodious voice.

Keen to find out what exactly was happening, he remained where he was in the anticipation she would come close enough for him to ask her. He was not to be disappointed. Indeed, she did more than come close, she came up to him, a highly attractive young woman in her early to middle twenties dressed in T-shirt and jeans, with lustrous black hair cascading down onto her shoulders – informal dress to be sure if she were a serious rider. For he had rarely seen anybody on horseback – man or woman – in these parts not dressed in the traditional white breeches, tight fitting black boots, black or red frock coat and hard hat.

"Afternoon," she said, brightly. "I'm looking for a lost dog – Bob's his name," she added with a wide smile, "though I'm sure that'll not surprise you."

"I've not seen a dog," he replied. "What sort is he?"

"A sheep dog – collie. Black and white. Not the rarest sort of animal around here, I must admit." The smile remained upon her face, and he realised just how pretty she was. Not beautiful – her features were a shade too small for that. But stunningly pretty. And obviously local born – the soft Devonshire burr in her slight accent betrayed as much.

"No, I'm sorry. I've not seen him. How long has he been missing?"

"Only since last night. There's probably nothing to worry about. He's probably gone courting. It's not like him, though. He's a real home-bird normally. So I thought it worthwhile to have an hour or two looking for him – and enjoy a ride in the sunshine at the same time."

"How far have you ridden?" asked the middle-aged man, quite enjoying this conversation with a good looking young woman. Few of those had crossed his path in recent times.

"Not far – I live at Bray Barton – a farm only about a mile from here. You might not know it if you've not lived here long, because you can't get to it on this road; you have to go further along the main road and then branch off."

"I've an idea I know where you mean. I think I've driven along that way but not for some time. I believe . . ." What George Tennant believed was not to be conveyed to his companion, for speech was snatched suddenly from him, along with sensibility. All he was aware of was a dying of the sunlight and all embracing darkness.

Chapter Two

Through the darkness he seemed to hear a voice – but was it real or imaginary? Slowly he knew it was real, and it was becoming louder. The blackness, too, began to ease itself into murky greyness then forward to a weak light.

"Are you all right?" The urgent question was asked in a tone suggesting deep concern, but no panic, and it was repeated many times. It was not a particularly sensible enquiry, though, for somehow he had the feeling he was not at all 'all right'. He felt a hand gently slapping his face, heard the voice rise to a higher pitch, felt warmth about him – and opened his eyes slowly to the light.

"Oh, thank heavens – you've come around," came a voice pregnant with relief. His charming acquaintance of but a few minutes knelt beside him gazing down at him anxiously. "I was so worried about you. Out like a light, you went. One minute you were talking, then the next you were collapsing to the ground."

"I'm sorry," he mumbled, pulling himself up into a sitting position.

"Nothing to be sorry about," she retorted. "I'm just a little concerned you fainted the way you did. For that's what it was, I expect – a faint. Has anything like this ever happened to you before?"

He shook his head. "Never. I'm fifty years old and I've never fainted before in my life."

"It must be the sight of me," she joked. "Actually you don't look at all well. I think a cup of tea would do you good. Shall I go into the house and make one?"

"Yes – yes, please do. The back door's open, and the kitchen is just inside to the right."

"Fine – I'll go in and make a pot."

"Thanks – thanks . . . of course, I don't know your name."

"Heather – Heather Maunder; a good name for a girl born and bred on the Moor, don't you think?" she giggled.

He smiled wanly and nodded. "It is that," he agreed.

She ran off towards the back of the house, whilst he pulled himself gingerly to his feet and ambled very slowly up the lawn to the picnic table where lay the remains of his lunch. He dropped heavily against the rather rough hewn bar at his back, and closed his eyes. He had no idea as to what had afflicted him, but he most definitely did not like it.

Within a few minutes Heather reappeared carrying a tray upon which lay two empty mugs, a milk jug, a bowl of sugar and a large teapot. "I found everything – as you can see," said she, cheerfully, as she approached the picnic table. She had soon placed the tray upon the rather uneven surface of the table, poured the tea, and sat down opposite her host.

"Is there anybody else in the house who should be told of your fainting?" she asked in her bright, forthright manner.

"Nobody – I live on my own."

"Oh – I see." There was surprise in her voice. "It's a huge house for just one. But then," she added hastily, "that's none of my business, Mr . . ."

"Tennant – George Tennant. Call me George," he said simply. "And seeing as you've been so kind to me this afternoon, Heather, there seems no reason for me not to tell you that I'm on my own because I'm a widower. I have been these past eighteen months or so. My wife, Janet, died some – what – probably just over two years after we moved down from London."

"How dreadful."

"Yes, it was. And totally unexpected. But such things happen, of course," he opined, with a false casualness which did not go unnoticed. His young and charming visitor sensed there was pain for him in this conversation.

"Is there anybody I can phone about your – your – your funny turn just now," she enquired solicitously.

"No thanks – nobody at all."

"How about the doctor?"

"Definitely not the doctor. They're fine people, and all that, but the less you see of them, the better."

11

"Well, in that case, is there anything I can do for you – anything I can get you?"

"No, Heather, thanks. I'll be all right now. Don't know what it was. Possibly the warm weather. Anyway, I doubt I'll have any more trouble."

"Good. Well, I'd better carry on looking for Bob."

She drained the tea from her mug, got up from her somewhat uncomfortable seat and looked down at her host. "Thanks for the tea George – and make sure you take care of yourself." She moved quickly across the wide lawn to the small gate which led onto the moorland, then over to her, obviously, elderly horse, busy cropping the wiry grass.

"Look in again if you're passing," the lonely householder called as she latched the gate behind her.

"I will – and sooner than you think. I've got to ride over this way on, probably, Thursday. We've some of our sheep on the moor about a mile or so up beyond here – those which haven't wandered off elsewhere can be found reasonably close together usually – so I ride up there at least once a week. I've been past here scores of times during the years you've been living here; it's amazing I've never seen you before."

With those words, she waved at the middle-aged man, turned – and was gone.

George watched her clamber, lithely, upon her horse and pass onwards in search of the errant dog. Despite his rather sinister loss of consciousness, it had been a most interesting day.

Chapter Three

Heather was as good as her word and duly appeared on the following Thursday – accompanied by Bob, who had returned home on the afternoon of the day she had met the widower.

George had to admit to himself that he had spent most of the time since their first meeting eagerly anticipating the event. And it was to be the first of many visits from the farmer's daughter throughout that summer – and beyond. Always once, sometimes twice a week she would appear, on her horse if the weather was dry, in a battered Land Rover if raining. She would usually arrive around lunch-time, insist that he sit and do nothing, then prepare a simple meal in the kitchen, which she soon knew intimately.

He had to confess that the attention of such a charming young woman flattered him immensely, but it also bemused him somewhat. Why did she wish to spend time with him, a man more than old enough to be her father. Indeed, so much did it intrigue him, he decided to ask her.

Her answer was simple, "Because I like coming over to see you and to talk. You are a very interesting man, you know, even though you are very sparing when it comes to telling me about your past – why you came here and so on."

"Me – sparing of information? What cheek," he rasped, with mock annoyance. "There's nobody more open than me when it comes to telling of the past," he continued, untruthfully. "After all, I've nothing to hide."

"Well, tell me about it then."

"There's not that much to tell, really. Janet and I had both lived in London all of our lives. In fact, she was a real Cockney – Bow Bells, and all that. We married young, had a couple of kids; I worked in the printing trade for several years and about fifteen years ago I set up my own business. And surprisingly – very surprisingly looking back – it went exceptionally well. So well, in fact, that about four years ago one of the big companies wanted to buy me out. I wasn't keen, feeling I was both too young – and too poor – to retire. But they made me an offer I couldn't refuse – as the saying goes. So I didn't. I just took the money – which was sufficient to retire on if we didn't go mad – and we came down here to live, Janet and me. The kids had grown up by then, of course, and left home. We had both got fed up with London, with the way it had changed – though, perhaps, it was us who had changed – and we both loved coming down to Devon on holiday. And Dartmoor held a special magic for us. Anyway, an estate agent sent us details of this house, we came down to see it, knew immediately it was the place for us and, seeing as we could afford it, bought it. And I think we would have lived here happily ever after, except that Janet up and died. A massive heart attack. And she had always been as healthy as a trout. Since then I've been a bit lost here, if truth be told. It's a beautiful house, mind you, and I still have a love affair with Dartmoor – but life gets just a touch lonely at times."

"Yes, it must do," agreed his visitor. "But don't you meet anybody in your work?"

"No – because I don't work. Not that I'm lazy, mind you," he added hastily, aware that a country born girl such as Heather would almost certainly have been imbued with the work ethic. "No, it's just that I invested the money from the sale of my business reasonably wisely and that pays me sufficient to keep body and soul together whilst I play around with my – my – well, my dream I suppose."

"Your dream?"

"To write a novel. I know it's the sort of thing many folk say and it could be I will never actually achieve it, but all my life I have wanted to write, Heather, but never had the time. Now I have all the time in the world; the trouble is I lack the inspiration. I keep writing opening chapters – then throw them into the bin, and start again. Frustrating, to say the least. If I'm honest with myself – and such a thing is never easy is it, being honest with oneself? – it is highly unlikely my novel will ever be anything more than a dream. Mind you, there's been plenty of other things to keep me busy. During virtually all the period since coming here

14

until Janet's death, there was always an enormous amount to do both inside the house and without; the place had been let go somewhat, as you probably know. Anyway we had broken the back of things before Janet died. If she had lived, I'm sure the entire place would be looking like a palace now. But when she went so much of my drive and focus went with her. I've been like a rudderless ship, unable to really concentrate on anything. This past eighteen months or so, have been more depressing and lonely than I can ever describe – and totally pointless and aimless."

"Then why have you stayed here?"

"I'm not sure I've anywhere else to go. Obviously I could move back to London, but I don't want to go back to that way of life again. Anyway, I wouldn't know anybody there now. I knew precious few when we left; I've always been a bit of a lone wolf."

"I can see I shall have to sort you out," quipped his companion.

"Well, that's a nice thought I must confess. The only worry I've got is that some burly boyfriend, or even husband, might come round to do the sorting out," he said, blatantly 'fishing'.

She laughed. "There's certainly no husband. I've not gone in for one of those yet. And no boyfriend either – at present."

"I find that difficult to believe," he cooed. "A lovely girl like you must have a queue of suitors."

"Suitors – that's a nice old-fashioned word," she mused. "I suppose I do have a few of those – but none I'd leave home for. In fact, it would take a very special kind of man to entice me away from home."

"That's a nice thing to say – and rarely heard these days."

"It just shows I'm a rather old-fashioned kind of girl," she replied, teasingly.

"You live on the farm with your mum and dad, do you?"

"With my dad and brother, actually – my mum died six years ago. So amongst other things, I keep house for them. My brother won't be home much longer, though. He's getting married and is going to live in a cottage in the village. So there'll be just Dad and me in that great big house then. Though, who knows, I might bring a husband home to help fill it," she added with a laugh.

"What would your father say then?"

"Oh, I think he would be delighted. He's always saying it's time I was married. 'Twenty-five years old and no husband; you'll end up an old maid,' that's what he says. He'd miss me, mind you, if I did get married and left home — both in the house and out on the farm; and he well knows it. But Dad's of that generation who feel that a woman is unfulfilled if she fails to land a husband, and he worries I'll miss out on something."

My generation, George thought to himself. "Do you think you are?" he asked.

"I doubt it; in fact, I doubt if I've missed out on anything up 'til now. Still, I'll probably marry some day, but he will have to be a bit special — and he will have to love the land."

"As you do," he stated simply.

"As yet, I've not met any man I have loved half as much as I love the farm, the livestock, and the moors."

"I reckon you will someday."

"We'll see."

The day he had this conversation with Heather was a stuffy Tuesday in late August and he was to wonder later that day whether or not her visits were affecting his health. For within half an hour of her leaving, following their light lunch, he fainted once again.

He had no way of knowing how long he was unconscious but felt it had been but a few minutes. But even if it had only been seconds, it was obvious there was something wrong with him and it was time he saw somebody about it.

Doctor Conway was a tall, heavily built man with a face so florid it appeared he was perpetually on the brink of a heart attack. Yet he was a keen golfer and was often to be seen jogging around the streets of Tavistock, so the threat of imminent illness did not appear to be a pressing problem for this able and genial man.

There was little evidence of geniality when he examined George Tennant, however. Just the opposite, in fact. For he invariably treated news of middle-aged men passing out with the utmost seriousness, and examined the patient from top to toe in an effort to find just what had caused the man to faint twice in a mere few weeks when he had never, in his entire life, passed out before. He was to come to no conclusions, however, except for those which were negative.

"Well, Mr Tennant, I can give you a list of ailments and diseases from which you are not suffering, but I cannot in honesty say with any degree of certainty what the problem is. Your heart is sound enough, you are not diabetic, you have not had a stroke – and it crossed my mind that you might have done – your blood pressure is normal. No, I cannot find a thing wrong with you. Yet you have passed out twice so there has to be something not right. Therefore I feel it best if I refer you to a neurologist in Plymouth, Doctor Worthington. He'll get to the bottom of it, you can be sure of that."

So it was that a bright, fresh October morning found George Tennant banished from the autumn sunshine, lying flat on a hospital bed, his head festooned with myriad electrodes which were attached to his sparsely haired scalp by what smelt, and felt, like super-glue. An EEG was the official abbreviation for what was being perpetrated upon his prostrate person – a means of measuring some sort of activity in the brain. Or, at least, that was about all he was able to gain from the rather uncommunicative technician who, seemingly efficiently, stuck the electrodes on his head and then, easier than he had anticipated, removed them again – an hour or so later.

After the EEG he was sent to wait his turn to see the impressively named Doctor Winston Worthington. That wait consumed some of the, generally, banal words contained in half a dozen uninspiring waiting-room magazines and over an hour of his time, but eventually his name was called and he found himself sitting before a fellow of some sixty years of age whose somewhat round shouldered rather spare frame was not in keeping with a man whose name promised strength and presence. There was about the consultant, however, a briskness of manner which suggested to George that he would not have to wait long for a diagnosis.

"Just run through the attacks for me if you would. The build up to them, what you can remember of them, how you felt afterwards and so on," he requested, in a soft, but authoritative tone of voice.

The patient did as he was bid, though there was little to tell as there did not appear to be any build up to the attacks, he did not know what was happening during them and had felt merely a little disorientated afterwards. No sooner had he finished his description, than the consultant was into a diagnosis.

"Yes, it is as I thought from what your GP has described in his

17

letter and from the results of the EEG; you are suffering from epilepsy." He paused, and gazed keenly at his patient, apparently anxious to see what reaction this pronouncement would bring.

George Tennant, essentially a phlegmatic man, reacted according to character.

"I see," he muttered, a puzzled though by no means worried expression flitting across his face. "What does that mean exactly? Do I have to have treatment?"

"Medication. Tablets to be exact. There are several drugs which will control epilepsy these days. It's just a matter of finding out which one does the trick as far as you are concerned. All totally painless, I'm glad to say."

"Well, that's good news, Doctor. No great hardship taking a few tablets every day – even if I have to do so for the rest of my life." He articulated the words in his normal, easy relaxed fashion, but was slowly becoming enveloped by the grip of feelings of acute unease. He could think of no logical reasons for it, but somehow the word 'epilepsy' held connotations of problems that had not yet manifested themselves. Within a few seconds, one had.

"Tell me, Mr Tennant – do you drive?" The Doctor asked the question in a conversational tone of voice, but his patient instantly felt such a probe had nothing to do with inconsequential pleasantries.

"Yes – yes I do. I have for thirty years or more. I drove down here today. It would be a major undertaking to get to Plymouth from where I live if I did not run a car."

"I'm sure it would." Doctor Worthington shook his head. "However, I am afraid you are going to have to face such an undertaking in future. You see, the law requires that a doctor or consultant inform the DVLC at Swansea if he or she diagnoses any patient as suffering from epilepsy. There is no option, sadly."

"And what happens then?" The question was staccato sharp, almost to the point of rudeness, but spoken in such a way because of the tightening and sudden dryness of the patient's throat.

"DVLC will write to you informing you that your licence has been revoked."

"For how long?"

"Well, the minimum period is two years. If you have no more attacks, then you can apply to have your licence reinstated two

18

years from the day of its revocation. Should you have further attacks, though, then the two year disqualification begins from the time of the most recent attack – obviously. So it is important we get you onto medication and stop these attacks as soon as possible. I will write to your GP – Doctor Conway I believe it is . . ."

The patient nodded confirmation.

"So, I will write to Doctor Conway giving him my diagnosis and recommendation as to the medication he should prescribe for you. The drug should prevent any further attacks, but I think it best if I keep an eye on you for the foreseeable future, so I'd be obliged if you would make an appointment on your way out to see me in approximately two months time. Any questions, anything you are uncertain about?"

"No – no, not really Doctor, thank you," replied George, softly, his mind giddy with bewilderment. "It's just that it's hard to take it all in – especially about the driving. Living where I do, I really do not know how I shall be able to cope if I'm unable to drive."

"Yes, it will be a problem, Mr Tennant. The driving ban is usually the main problem for most epileptics. Tell me, do you rely on your car to take you to work – or, even worse, do you drive for a living?"

"Oh no, nothing like that. I'm semi-retired really. No job depends on my licence. It's just the damned inconvenience of it all."

"I can see that, and sympathise fully," agreed the consultant, briskly. "Still, I have to say you are better off than a goodly number of people who come to me. So many rely on driving to earn their crust; by being instrumental in depriving them of their licence, I am also taking their living. I invariably feel guilty."

"A fair point Doctor. Such folk are far worse off than me, without a doubt. But it's still a damned nuisance."

"Indeed it is," he replied, as he got up from his swivel chair, moved from behind his desk, walked briskly to the door and opened it. "Now, if you will make that appointment as I said just now and, also, go to your own doctor in about ten days time. By then, he will have received my letter so will be in a position to prescribe the drugs which should stop these wretched attacks."

"Very well, Doctor – and thank you," replied the patient, a touch of despair in his voice.

He went down the corridor to the reception desk, made an appointment for two months hence as instructed, then meandered slowly out of the hospital and into the road adjoining, where was parked his Jag. He unlocked the door, clambered inside, and slumped behind the wheel. And no sooner had he done so than it occurred to him that he would not be doing so for much longer. In fact, he had a feeling he should not be doing so now. What, after all, if he had an attack whilst driving home?

Yet, Doctor Worthington had not told him to stop driving immediately – and a wink was as good as a nod, as the saying went. So he leant forward, put the key into the ignition, turned on the engine, clipped in his seat belt, and moved out into the traffic. He was a law abiding man and would stop driving the very minute he was told to officially – but he would continue to operate his beloved Jaguar right up until the very last second of that unforgiving minute.

Chapter Four

The speed with which officialdom moved astonished George Tennant. When running his business, he had been used to various official organisations taking an inordinately long period of time to do the simplest things, but DVLC were obviously very different indeed. For it seemed to him that no sooner had they heard from Doctor Worthington than they put a letter in the post telling him that, regretfully, they had no option but to revoke his licence.

Thus it was he awoke one rainy morning at the end of October knowing that wherever he wanted to go that day – and for the foreseeable future – he would have to walk as he was no longer the possessor of a licence to drive. It seemed to be one of the worst moments of his life – though, in reality, he had known greater calamity and tragedy – for he felt a prisoner in a large, lonely house set miles from civilisation, in a landscape which, at its best had a wild, breathtaking beauty, but which, for very long periods of the years, was wet, bleak and strangely intimidating.

Yet, it was to prove very much an open prison – thanks to the beguiling young woman who, for reasons best known to herself, had befriended him when the days had been longer and nights shorter. Heather was to prove to be his salvation during that protracted winter. She became a daily visitor bringing gossip and bubbly chatter; a 'motivator', getting him to set to and do the decorating and repairs to the house which the damp and cold moorland climate made an almost unending chore; the creator of many culinary delights in his spacious kitchen – which made a welcome change from his own dire efforts of chips with everything – and, possibly most important of all, she proved to be a most able, and thoughtful taxi driver.

The vehicles which she drove were either her Land Rover or

his Jag, but she would always make time to drive him into Tavistock, or even Plymouth, for any appointments he might have, whilst his ride into Tavistock on the Friday Market day to do his weekly shopping became a regular event.

They soon settled into the routine of visiting a pub on the way home after their shopping trips – which George enjoyed very much and began to look forward to. Not that he drank much; indeed, he was not supposed to drink at all with the medication he was taking, though he figured that a couple of whiskies every week would do him no harm, whilst Heather, like most younger folk, always had the breathalyser in mind.

Yet both found this regular Friday interlude – which usually included a pub-lunch – a time of relaxation and, perhaps, even gentle courtship. Not that George would consider that there was, or ever could be, anything more between himself and this vivacious young farmer's daughter than a warm, mutually fulfilling friendship. After all, he was more than twice her age. In fact, at twenty-five she was younger than his own son and daughter. Yet he had to admit to himself that if their friendship suddenly ended, then life would be barren for him in the extreme, even if he were to have his driving licence restored and did not need her as a chauffeuse.

Seemingly, they talked of everything during those Friday lunch-times. George of the past – in accordance with his age and his nature – and of his two children, Martin who was twenty-eight and ran his own small engineering business in Brighton, and Alison, who was twenty-six and a teacher, married to a quantity surveyor living in Guildford. He spoke also, in almost reverential tones, of his grandson Jimmy, whom he had last seen at Christmas, having spent the yuletide with Martin and his wife Sylvia in their lovely bungalow overlooking the sea.

"I wish he lived a little nearer," he would say, wistfully – and often.

"That would be nice," Heather had replied on one occasion, "but only if they came to live near you. I wouldn't want you to go away to live near them. I'd miss you too much."

The words had been said in a casual, matter of fact way, but they had meant a great deal to George Tennant; the feeling that a lovely young woman would miss him fed his vanity and warmed his rather lonely heart.

22

Heather, for her part, chattered away about many things when they were together. About the farm, and her father and brother; about the gossip she had heard — and about her various boyfriends. And there always seemed to be a few of those about — much to George's chagrin. Yet he realised after a while that whilst she liked a lot of young men, she loved none — which placated him enormously. Indeed, no boyfriend seemed to last a fortnight before Heather was getting bored with him.

"He's so juvenile," she would say — invariably and universally.

"Well, you certainly can't say that about me," he had replied on one occasion when she had uttered the phrase with her usual amused exasperation.

"No, that's true," she had agreed. "Thank heavens, I say. I like a man to be mature. To know and to have known, and seen, something of life and the world."

He often thought of those words when he was alone in his big house; for they warmed him, made him feel of some account and importance in the world again — and he had not felt such personal esteem, probably, since he had retired; certainly not since Janet's death. Not that he spent a vast amount of time in his draughty home. Bray Barton was the place on which he passed a goodly portion of most days, helping Heather, her father Arthur and brother Derek, with the myriad and seemingly never ending tasks that forever makes farming such a hard master.

Arthur had been a little wary of this Cockney stranger for a while. Not that he had anything against him, but he had the countryman's inherent suspicion of anybody who could be classed as a 'townie', and also — and probably more importantly — he was not at all sure of the relationship between his daughter and this man who was a couple of years older than himself. He soon satisfied himself, though, that theirs was nothing more than a good, fulfilling friendship, and that the Londoner was not after his daughter. As time went on, however, and his opinions of George rose significantly, he had to admit to himself that it would not worry him greatly if something more than friendship did evolve between the middle-aged former businessman and Heather — since the death of his wife, the sole jewel of his existence.

And, also, he found George a considerable help about the farm. Not that the 'townie' possessed any country skills, but he was a willing labourer – and anxious to learn. The long moorland winter had seen him feeding the Maunder's large numbers of stock and sheep, driving fodder laden trailers across the peaty fields – where the lack of a driving licence was no handicap – to bring succour to the long horned, shaggy haired cattle and rugged sheep brought down from the higher moors in the late autumn, lending a hand with the repairing of hedges and dry stone walls, and performing the numerous other finger-freezing tasks that afflict farmers during the short days.

And the winter having passed, he became involved in the major harvest of the year for those who farmed in the foothills of the high, barren plateau – lambing. The Maunders kept a flock of almost one thousand breeding ewes, and whilst the stock bred from the moorland cattle was a significant source of income to them, it was the lambing which was the vital economic occurrence of the year.

A good lambing season, with a healthy crop of sturdy progeny and little loss of life amongst the ewes, would mean a reasonably happy bank manager for the rest of the year. Anything less, although not necessarily catastrophic, would put pressures on Arthur Maunder in terms both of finance and self-esteem. For he prided himself on being a good farmer and a poor lambing would invariably cause him to question his performance in his profession – a judgement not necessarily fair, but one inevitable in such a conscientious man born and bred to the moor.

There was no question of self doubt on the farmer's part during this spring however. For the lambing was excellent – "best for years," as Arthur readily admitted – and spirits generally at Bray Barton were as high as they could be. And this was not only due to the good news from the lambing pens; Derek's wedding, due at the end of May, was also a source of general happiness and antici-pation – especially on Heather's part. For she and her affable brother – who had become great friends with George, delighted to have another, and willing, pair of hands on the farm – were very close, and although only two years his senior, she fussed over him and his forthcoming betrothal as much as would any mother.

She joined with Elaine, Derek's fiancée, and her mother – who both lived in Peter Tavy – in making arrangements for the wedding, helped with the making of the bridesmaids' dresses, one of which she would be wearing herself, and threw herself into the multitude of tasks which invariably preceded such an event with an enthusiasm and effort which began to take their toll. So much so, in fact, that by the end of the first week in May, she began to look weary and just a little unwell.

It was when he saw her looking thus one morning, that George Tennant decided she needed a change of some sort – even if only a very brief one. So he phoned the best restaurant in the district – well, the most expensive, anyway – booked a table for two for the following Saturday night, and then confronted Heather with his action one bright morning as he helped her move a flock of sheep and lambs from a meadow near the house, to a field at the far end of the farm adjoining the moors, the penultimate move before being turned out onto the moor itself for the summer.

"What are you doing Saturday evening, Heather," he enquired, feeling much like a gauche schoolboy seeking a date with the prettiest girl in the class – and sounding much like it as well.

"Saturday evening? Let's see now – I think I'm going to the cinema in Plymouth with Johnny Willmott. You know him – he and his dad keep the garage in the village, although he does most of it now, his father being semi-retired because of poor health."

"Oh – yes, I know who you mean," replied George Tennant, trying, unsuccessfully, to keep the disappointment out of his voice.

"Why do you ask?" there was a forced casualness about Heather's question.

"Well, if you were free, I was going to suggest that I take you out to dinner – as – as a small token of my appreciation for all you've done for me these past six months and more. But if you've already arranged something then perhaps we could go out some other time."

"Oh, no – I've not really arranged anything for Saturday. It's just that when I was in the pub a couple of nights ago, Johnny asked me if I'd like to go to the pictures with him on that evening, and I said I would if I didn't have anything else on. But there's nothing definite about it. I'm supposed to phone him this evening to make arrangements. But if you're asking me out to dinner, then my answer is definitely, yes. I love good food – and good company," she added, warmly.

So it was that the following Saturday evening found George Tennant waiting, nervously, at the front door of his house for his

25

b

chauffeuse to arrive to take him out to dinner with her. And never had he felt, throughout his entire and not uneventful life, the way he felt at that moment. Here he was, a man well into middle age – and looking it – a grandfather, in uncertain health, with obviously the best and most productive years of his life behind him, waiting for a vivacious young woman to take him out on a date. At best the situation was bizarre – at worst, absurd.

And as he stood there in the fading evening sunshine, his uncertainty over his relationship with Heather Maunder began to turn to panic. How had he got himself into a position like this? A man his age involved with – well, with a young girl, almost. Janet would often use the saying – when men of his age did something stupid in their personal lives – that 'there's no fool like an old fool,' and he would sagely nod his agreement. Now it was he who was the fool. Yet, perhaps there was still time to put it all in reverse. Perhaps if he phoned Heather that minute and told her he was not feeling well and couldn't go out this night. Yes, that was what he would do. If he was quick, he might catch her before she left home.

But no – he was too late. For his milky white Jaguar was already on the way up the short drive to the house, with Heather – who by now, with George's encouragement, treated the car almost as her own – at the wheel. He stood rooted to the spot as the sleek car purred to a halt just a few feet in front of him, and its driver alighted.

And at that moment all thought of feigning illness deserted him along with the apprehension which had been wreaking its mischief within him. For standing before him was as lovely a young woman as he could ever recall seeing in his life. Clad in a tight fitting, yet demure green dress, her black hair cascading down onto her shoulders, her pretty face enhanced to loveliness by an astute, but sparing, use of make-up, she looked stunning – and he felt a man totally, but happily, out of his depth.

Chapter Five

That evening was amongst the best he had spent in years; for Heather was not merely so very good to look at, she was, as always, full of chatter and life – a totally positive person in the somewhat negative world in which he lived. Certainly before the evening was through, he had to acknowledge a factor which he had long suspected – that he was totally besotted with her.

The difference in their ages was suddenly irrelevant in his eyes; he knew now that his life, partially empty since he had retired from his business, totally so since the death of Janet, would remain so unless Heather became a permanent part of it. Yet it was all impossible. She was as sought after a young woman as could be found in the district, whilst he was a none too good product of a different generation. Still, she obviously enjoyed his company, for if she did not, then why did she seek it so often? Certainly she appeared to enjoy their evening together, as they laughed and talked their way through an excellent meal and emptied two bottles of wine – most of it being quaffed by him, as she was driving, a factor which, allied to his medication, made him feel more than a little tight. In fact, he became sufficiently inebriated not to have a totally clear recollection of the latter part of the evening, but he did remember, with blinding clarity, that as he was about to take his leave of her – and the Jag – at the front door of his house, she leant across from the driver's seat and planted a long though gentle kiss full upon his lips.

The first thing he thought of the following morning, and during the days which followed, was that kiss. Yet, so long had it been since he had last been involved in this courtship business, he was not really sure what it meant. He seemed to recall that in his youth such a kiss from a girl would signal that she saw the relationship as being more than friendship.

Yet, in more recent times, younger folk seemed to kiss more readily and, thus, it all held much less relevance. In fact, he could remember Martin and Alison bringing home girl and boy friends with whom their relationship was almost certainly platonic, yet whom they would invariably greet, or leave, with kisses and embraces. Perhaps that was the key to it all. Indeed, that was almost certainly it. Heather liked him, there was no doubt about that, but she almost certainly saw him as a sort of genial 'uncle' figure; or, perhaps, even worse, she was sorry for him – his loneliness and isolation, his inability to drive himself. Yes, that was probably it – or so he convinced himself within a few days of that wonderful Saturday night out. And it was a conviction which depressed him more than he would care to admit.

A day was to come, though, a mere fortnight after that night, when he was to make the exhilarating discovery that his conviction regarding Heather's feelings towards him was gloriously wrong. That day was a good one for the Maunder family, as it was the one on which Derek entered into matrimony at Peter Tavy Church, and celebrated the event at a reception at a hotel in Tavistock. Heather, once again, looked divine, her light purple bridesmaid's dress making her appear even younger than usual – and George felt guilty as he was aware that a wedding guest should really spend more time gazing at the bride.

It was an excellent day of good friendship, good will, humour and love, which not even the stormy late May weather could spoil, and George had to admit he felt disappointed when it all came to an end. Yet, the termination of the wedding celebrations proved not to be the end of the day by any means. For as he sat beside Heather – still clad in her bridesmaid's outfit – in the Jag as she drove back towards the moors, she suggested they stopped at their usual Friday lunchtime pub for a couple of drinks to end a near perfect day. He readily agreed.

The pub lounge was alive with its customary Saturday night business, yet Heather managed to find a couple of seats in the corner whilst George got the drinks – a fruit juice for him, as he had already had vastly more to drink at the reception than would be approved of by his doctor, and a coke for her, the drink driving laws still disciplining her mind despite the gentle euphoria of the day.

For a while they said very little, both seemingly relaxing after hours of rather exhausting jollification. Heather was the first to speak.

"Do you know, George, I've truly enjoyed today. It was lovely."

"It certainly was," he agreed. "As good a wedding as I've been to in many years. 'Course you never know with weddings. I've been to as many boring ones as I've been to enjoyable ones."

"Oh yes, that's quite true. I've been to some awful weddings. Yet, it's nothing to do with how much is spent on it or anything like that, is it?"

"No, that's right. It's more to do with the mix of people – how much genuine goodwill there is in the air, and so on."

"And how much love, George," said Heather, softly. "I felt there was a lot of love in both the church and the hotel today. Derek and Elaine love each other dearly, of course; worship each other, in fact. It's wonderful to see them. Childhood sweethearts, they were. Met at Tavistock School, and have been courting ever since. If they don't make a go of it, then nobody will."

"I fancy you're right. Mind you, most folk still make a go of marriage. The divorce rate is woefully high, of course, but even then the number of couples who stay together throughout their lives is far higher."

"Like you and Janet."

"Yes – that's right."

"She died so young, though, George. Do you ever feel bitter about it?"

"Not now. I did for a while; very bitter in fact. We had a good marriage, because we were always good friends, so when she died I felt probably almost as much loneliness as I did grief. But these past few months, I feel very much better about it all. Not that I'll ever forget her; she was too good a person ever to forget. But now I find myself looking more to the future than to the past – which is not really my nature. And it's all happened Heather since – since . . ." He stumbled over his words and looked away from her.

"It's all happened," he continued, "since I met you. I have to say that these past few months, helping you at Bray Barton, going out with you in the Jag or the Land Rover, have been as happy as any I can ever recall. I don't know what I shall do when they end." No sooner had the words left his lips than he regretted them.

He had never used emotional blackmail against anybody in his life, and it was no time to start now.

Whether or not Heather saw his words in such a light, however, he would never know, but her reply was so happily positive that he thought it unlikely she had. "Why should they end, George? Is there anything you haven't told me; have you found another woman or something?"

He grinned broadly. "Good God, no. How could I ever find any other woman who could compare with you?"

"Quite right," she retorted — then burst into laughter. She reached over and took his right hand in hers. "You do say some funny things, you know."

She leant forward in her seat and gazed into his eyes. "Can't you see, George, that I am in love with you — deeply in love. I won't say it was love at first sight, but I found you very interesting from that marvellous day when I was out on the moor looking for Bob. And since then my love for you has grown day by day. You are such a good man, George; kind, compassionate, courageous in your own way — and, may I say, very good looking."

"But, for heaven's sake, I'm twice your age. I'm older than your own father, Heather."

"That doesn't bother me. Anyway, you're not old, George. What's fifty or so? No age at all. What you are is mature — and I like men to be mature; to have experience of life and the world and of people. I couldn't bear to spend the rest of my life with anybody of my own age that I've ever met — but I would certainly be willing to spend it with you."

The words were plainly spoken and plainly meant, and George Tennant, usually a slow and cautious man, this time acted without hesitation. "Then I hope you will spend the rest of your life with me, Heather. I would be honoured, my dear, if you would agree to marry me," he said, both gravely and rather pompously.

Heather laughed. "That sounded like something out of Dickens, George. You're not that old, surely?" She leant forward at the same time, pulled him gently towards her across the small table, and kissed him.

"I do agree to marry you, George — and the sooner the better."

Chapter Six

For several days after his proposal to Heather, George Tennant was not really himself. Not that he was ill; rather, if truth be told, he was gripped by a form of panic. That he loved this farmer's daughter, he could not deny; that he wanted to be with her constantly, was a simple fact. But it had all happened so suddenly; possibly, for the first time in his life, his heart had ruled his head, and that alarmed him.

Despite this, deep down within him, he knew that his impulse had been correct. For he had not the slightest doubt that marriage to Heather would bring back joy and fulfilment to his life. Yet he was not a selfish man, and there lay the problem. For he was not at all sure he should have asked this lovely young woman to be his wife. Granted, she had almost forced him to do so, but that was no real excuse. For there was a factor in their relationship which was obviously of massive importance – the twenty-six years gap in their ages.

Heather said it did not concern her. In fact, she looked upon it as an advantage. Yet, had she thought it through? After all, when she reached her forties – and was still a young woman – he would be an old man; he might even be dead. And they were not of the same generation – thus inevitably looking differently at life, and having different attitudes and priorities. Would it work out? Would he make her happy? Essentially a cautious, even pessimistic man, the more he thought of it, the less he was convinced that he would.

And he voiced these fears to Heather a couple of weeks after the proposal. That fine June morning found the two of them on horseback up on the high moors, officially checking there were no problems amongst the sheep and the shaggy moorland cattle –

or, at least, those they were able to find – which would stay up on the heather, fern and bracken encrusted plateau until the autumn. If ever there was a place conducive to talk of love and marriage then this was it.

Not that it was a romantic spot. Romance was no part of the magic of Dartmoor. At its worst, it was a grim, grey, intimidating wilderness, where man, even at his most sophisticated, was but a pawn to the weather, the altitude and the unyielding, rock ridden, uncultivatable soil. At its best, though, it was magnificent – and this crystal clear morning, with a fresh westerly wind countering the heat of the mid-summer sun, was as good a day as Dartmoor could ever produce. The couple moved slowly across the spongy plateau between two high tors, the vista to their left including Tavistock, the City of Plymouth and the sea beyond.

Heather brought her horse to a stop, and her future husband did likewise – or, rather, the old mare he was riding decided to follow suit. This horse riding business was still an art a long way from being accomplished as far as George Tennant was concerned. Heather gazed down at the lowland country, then, with a sweep of her arm in its general direction, made the statement of a natural born countrywoman; "It's going to rain."

"Rain? Get on – there's not a cloud in the sky."

"Things are too clear for it to be settled, George. There's no haze. Look, you can see ships out near the Eddystone Lighthouse, and that's a good thirty miles away. It'll rain before nightfall."

George smiled then shook his head. "I'll not argue with you, my love," he replied. "You're usually right about weather."

"I ought to be; I've spent most of my life out in it – and Dartmoor weather's not like any other. It's certainly not like London weather," she added, with a laugh.

"That's true," he agreed. "I've never been as cold in my life as I was the first winter we were down here. I've got a little more used to it now, but I do wish we had just a touch more sunshine. I reckon my blood's a bit thin – to do with my age, I expect."

"What nonsense," came the sharp retort. "You're not very old."

"But I am – compared to you. And it worries me; it worries me all the time." He turned in his saddle and looked at his companion. "I love you dearly, Heather – and I'm sure you know that. But the difference in our age is enormous – more than a quarter of a century. When you are still a young woman, I shall

32

be an old man. In fact, to put it brutally, I might well be dead. And if – and if we were to have children . . ."

"I certainly hope we do," she interjected. "I want two or three kids about the place. A girl to be a friend to her mum, and perhaps a couple of boys to help on the farm – that's if we are still on the farm once we're married. I certainly hope so." The words were spoken with some urgency – the farm, and the way of life which it begot, was extremely important to Heather.

Her companion shrugged his shoulders. "I hadn't thought about our future at all. Everything has happened so quickly, that's the trouble."

"Trouble?" she exclaimed.

"Well no – no – of course not. Just the opposite, in fact. What it is, though, is that I'm just a bit bowled over by everything. Just think, my dear, that a few months ago I was a retired, widowed businessman leading a quiet, secluded life in the country, with my future, though boring, totally certain, whilst now I don't know if I'm coming or going. I need to settle my mind a bit – and make some decisions about the future."

"Well, you've made the main one, George," retorted his delightful companion in her brisk and bubbly way. "The main question now, to my way of thinking, is when you're going to do the deed."

"Deed?"

"Don't be thick – marry me, of course." There was exaspera-tion in her voice; he could certainly be obtuse at times. "It's time we set the date, George – and decided where we're going to live, amongst other things. And all your nonsense about being too old and such-like only comes in the way of deciding the important things. So please, no more tripe about you being too old for me. You're the man I love, the man I shall marry and the man I intend to spend the rest of my life with – all right?"

He laughed, then nodded his head. "Yes – all right," he agreed. "I'll say no more about it if you don't want me to. It's only that the age difference between us has worried me somewhat, and . . ."

She stilled his voice with a glare, he dropping the reins and raised his hands like someone in the act of surrender. "All right," he complied. "I'll say no more about it, not now or ever."

"Good. Now let's get down to important matters – like arrangements."

33

They went some considerable way towards mapping out their future life together as they rode across the moors, each casting the perfunctory glance at the odd sheep or long-haired bullock that came into view. The wedding, they decided, would be on the first Saturday in October – "Rather quick," George had said in his cautious way, only to be put in his place by a brisk, "Nonsense, it's almost four months away" – at Peter Tavy Church, with the reception at the Russell Hotel in Tavistock.

"What if it's not convenient to the vicar or the hotel," had been the comment of the pessimistic George. He had been countered, though, by a positive response.

"It's convenient – I've already checked. And I've already booked the church and hotel for that day – the church for noon."

After more discussion, it was decided they should live in George's house on the hill, although much of their time would no doubt be spent at Bray Barton. It had been a difficult decision for Heather to make – and George had left it to her as her position was far more complex than his. To a girl with the traditional upbringing that was hers, the notion of her husband providing the home after marriage was the correct one. In this instance, however, things were a little different.

For she had kept house for her father for so long she felt a certain obligation towards him. He had lost his wife, to whom he had been devoted, and now, within the space of a third of a year, was to lose his son and daughter to wedlock. Bray Barton farmhouse was awfully big for just one man. With all this in mind, Heather had sat down with him and discussed the situation just a few days after having told her father of her intention to marry George Tennant. That news had shocked Arthur Maunder at first. Not that he had anything against the Londoner; the opposite, in fact, for he had developed a high opinion of the retired businessman who spent so much time at Bray Barton, seeing him as being a man of both integrity and worth – indeed, a gentleman.

"Mind you, it'll be a day or two before he makes a farmer," he would say, many a time, in the bar of the village pub, when making his regular Saturday night visit.

But the thought of him – a man older than himself – marrying his beloved daughter, really concentrated his mind. Not that he was a possessive man and didn't want her to make her own life, in her own way. On the contrary, he welcomed it; for Heather had so much to give to any relationship and was a born homemaker. The man marrying her would be fortunate; indeed he was not at all sure that he had met anyone worthy of such a prize – a point he put with customary directness to his daughter when she had told him of her love for, and intention to marry, George.

But that direct opinion was quickly used by his quick witted daughter to put her father on the defensive. "You're right to a large extent – I do deserve the best, Dad. And Mum would say the same were she here now, of that I'm sure. But George is the best. Or let me put it another way, Dad; you've got to know George very well during the past few months with him becoming so involved with the farm, and I can tell you have formed a high opinion of him and that you like him very much. His only drawback is that he knows little about farming in general and nothing about moorland farming in particular. Now, you've also known a whole drove of young local fellows who have come here to court me, or to try, over the past half dozen years. Most of them know a lot more about farming than George does, but who would you rather I married – him, or one of that self-centred, empty-headed lot."

"Oh, I'm not saying anything against George," her father had said without hesitation. "He is a man I like, as you said – and a man I respect."

"And how many of the others do you respect?"

The farmer shrugged his shoulders. "I can't really say, maid. I don't know them that well."

"Oh, come on Dad. A goodly number of them you've known since they were 'cheels'. The truth is, you can't really tell one from the other – which is fair enough, because I can't either. They're all the same; all they want from a night out with a woman is beer and bed. Not that they got very far with me," she added hastily. "But George is different – and I'm sure that, really, you recognise that. He's kind, generous, courteous, respectful – Dad, he's a gentleman, and the day he marries me, I shall be the world's happiest woman."

Her father was silent for a few seconds, gazing down at the almost empty teacup sitting on its saucer on the large kitchen table in front of him. Then, his thought processes over, and a decision reached, he leant back in his hard chair and gazed up at his daughter. "You're right, maid, he is a gentleman, and if I'm honest with myself, I know he'll make you very happy. It's just the age difference that's worried me – naturally enough; I'm sure you understand that. But I reckon you've both thought about that, and considered it – so there's no more to be said. Be happy maid, that's the main thing. You deserve it."

Heather had bent over and kissed him, then, wiping away her tears – it had been an emotional moment – had suggested she make another cup of tea. That made, and partly drunk, she came round to the subject of where she and her new husband were going to live. She had barely got into the subject, though, before Arthur Maunder had suggested the solution – though perhaps dictated would be a more accurate word. When Heather had voiced her indecision (an untruth on her part as she and George had already decided to reside at his home) as to whether she should live in George's house or whether her new husband should move into Bray Barton, so that she could keep house for them all, he had spoken simply – the collective wisdom of generations of countrymen in his blood; "A woman should always live in her husband's house. There he's master – here, I am; and he'll not like that if he's the man I think he is."

"But who'll care for you," his daughter had protested.

"I can look after myself, maid," he had replied. "Anyway, it's not as if you'll be far away if I need you. And I expect you'll still spend a fair bit of your time here at Bray Barton, won't you?" The last sentence was said with a little urgency, for whilst Arthur Maunder felt that he could muddle through in the house without his daughter, to be able to do so outside was a very different matter indeed.

He had no cause for concern. "Of course I will, Dad. Most of every day I expect; I couldn't imagine life without Bray Barton. And George as well. He enjoys farming you know – and he's beginning to learn a bit about it, too."

"But won't George have to get a job. I mean, he'll have a wife to support now – and they don't come cheap," he said with a rare smile.

"He's got a lot of investments, Dad, which pay out fairly well – but, having said that, you might well be right. He's only had himself to keep in recent years; with me and – well, there could be others – it won't be so easy for him. Mind you, I don't really

36

know what his personal position is, but there aren't many folk about these days who can survive without working. He has spoken of writing a novel, but I doubt he ever will. He's too practical and restless a man to have the discipline to be able to sit down and write thousands of words."

"Perhaps we can arrange something here, Heather; George has certainly been a master help these past few months and there's too much really for Derek, you and myself with the extra yaws and bullocks we've got now."

"Do you know, Dad, I think he would like that. Like so many people who've spent most of their lives in a big city, he loves the country and thinks Bray Barton is heaven on earth. And he would be a great help."

"We'll work something out, maid. I'll have a word with Derek and see what he thinks. Obviously he's got to be paid, so I'll have to have a chat with the accountant as well. 'Course, being married to you – and you being a partner in the place – he'll be a sort of partner as well."

So it was formally acknowledged by all concerned that they would live at George's and would continue to work at Bray Barton, and get paid for it.

George readily and happily agreed to what had been arranged between Heather and her father, the prospect of working full-time at Bray Barton strangely pleasing him more than the fact that, when married, they should live in his house. For he enjoyed working on the farm, no matter what the task or the time of year.

Whether it was helping with the lambing or taking out fodder to the stock on a freezing winter's day, or, as he was now doing, helping with haymaking under the relentless heat of the summer sun, he felt a type of freedom which he had never known before. And whilst, physically, the work was harder than anything he had ever done, it was, to him, virtually without stress. And Arthur Maunder's proposal that he be paid for his labours also pleased him, for with a wife to help support he would have to ensure that he had a regular income above and beyond the dividends he derived from his investments.

The one worry which he had during this long, lovely summer, the end of which would see him a husband once again, was how to tell his son and daughter – and what their reaction would be. Not that he couldn't guess. Martin, to whom he had always been

37

very close, might well have doubts about his father marrying a woman even younger than he was, but would never dream of saying it. Rather, he would express delight that his father would have somebody with whom he could share his large house, and genuinely wish him well.

Alison's reaction, though, would not be the same. She was very different from her brother and George had to admit that he had never got on with her as well as he would have liked. Not that they had ever really argued or had any major disputes, but he had never felt in tune with her. And it had been so since she was a small child. Always she had had a better relationship with her mother, though why, he had never understood. Possibly there was a natural affinity between them. Both were brisk, sharp people — something which he had never been. And both could, at times, have a somewhat wounding tongue, though Janet had possessed a wit lacking in her daughter. Also Alison's job as a school teacher had tended, in the past few years, to make her somewhat opinionated and bossy. He had a feeling that from his daughter, when he informed her of his forthcoming marriage, there would be a lecture.

Still, the job had to be done and as it was information which could not really be imparted by letter, nor even by phone, he decided to go up to the south-east and tell them face to face – and take Heather with him. Her presence on the occasion would have a three-fold advantage; she would be excellent company on the journey, he would be able to introduce her to his children personally – her vivacious charm surely helping to draw the teeth of any criticism which might come his way – and, finally, and infinitely important, Heather would be able to do the driving.

So it was that a dull, thundery Saturday morning at the end of July saw the couple heading up the motorway on their journey to Guildford where Martin lived. They were to stay the night with him, then travel to Brighton to see Alison on the Sunday morning, returning the long journey home that evening.

It was to be a weekend which went largely in the direction which George thought it would, but was in reality, rather worse. Martin and his pretty, plumpish, likeable wife Sylvia, along with his grandson, Jimmy, greeted them warmly – and genuinely so as well, George had no doubt of that. And that warmth did not cool in the slightest degree during their stay. His son and daughter-in-law welcomed the news of his forthcoming marriage to Heather with the delight which he expected they would show, and he had no reason to feel it was anything other than totally sincere.

They certainly seemed to take to Heather – but then, he mused to himself, who wouldn't. The only aspect of their stay which caused George any worry was the revelation by Martin that he was having major business problems.

"High interest rates, bad debts, a slackening off of business – you know how it is, Dad," he said with a depressing simplicity. George did, indeed, know how it was – though he had always managed to avoid the worst ravages of such a situation.

Whether or not Martin would, however, remained to be seen. If the son failed, though, there was a problem for the father. For when Martin had set up in business some four years previously, George had stood guarantor at the bank to a sum of one hundred and fifty thousand pounds. At the time, with business booming, being guarantor to a son who had a very wise head on his shoulders despite his youth, seemed little more than being party to a trifling, and largely irrelevant piece of red tape on the part of the bank. Now, though, the calling in, by the bank, of the guarantee was a real possibility, and Martin, in his straightforward way, did not hesitate to inform his father of the situation – albeit with profound, and heartfelt apologies, for putting him in such a position. It was a situation which greatly concerned the older man, largely because his investments and savings in total were little more than half the one hundred and fifty thousand pounds which would be needed. But that, he reasoned, was tomorrow's problem – and hopefully in this direction, tomorrow would never come.

Despite the worry concerning Martin's business, the visit to him and Sylvia was a great success, for Heather had been accepted by both George's son and daughter-in-law – indeed, welcomed by them, as being a most suitable wife for a father for whom they had much love and respect. The visit to Alison, though, was somewhat less successful.

Though welcomed courteously by both she and her husband, Simon – basically a pleasant, easy-going young man, but one who invariably took his lead from his wife – both George and Heather felt on edge during the six hours they were at the house in

Brighton. Yet it was not only the visitors, but the hosts also who appeared unable to relax. And the main reason was simply the unease between Alison and her father. Neither could explain it any more than they could have done down the years, but now that they rarely saw each other, the intangible tension between them had strengthened.

Heather and George's afternoon at Brighton though, seemed to go tolerably well with everyone making an effort to be pleasant to everyone else. The damage, however, was done as the final curtain was about to fall on their visit. Having partaken of an excellent tea, they all got up from the table and followed Simon out into the garden where he was going to ask Heather's advice – for she was a consummate gardener – on an azalea which was looking a little jaded. The two of them went down to the far end of the garden to see the shrub, leaving Alison and George standing together on the small patio outside the back door.

"She seems very pleasant, Dad," said his daughter in a rather flat tone of voice when her husband and future mother-in-law were out of ear-shot.

"She is Alison – that and much more."

"I've got to say though, Dad, that she's extremely young. I shouldn't think she's any older than me."

"She's not – a year younger, in fact."

"That's what I thought." She took her gaze from Heather and looked at her father. "Have you thought this through, Dad. Oh, I know it must be very flattering to have a pretty young thing like that chasing you when you're well into middle age, but have you really thought of all the problems you'll face. Heaven knows, marriage is difficult enough for people of the same age, but when there's the age gap there is between you two, then the problems are enormous."

"And how would you know, Alison," asked her father, tersely, making a valiant effort to keep his temper.

"It's obvious, Dad, isn't it. Marriage between different generations is surely like marriage between different races – fraught with trouble."

"So you don't think it will last, then?"

"That's not for me to say, Dad. But I do think I have a right to pass comment on it," she said sharply, aware of the annoyance in his voice. "I am your daughter after all."

"Quite so. And I'm your father – and I thought you would wish me happiness for the future."

"I do, Dad – of course I do. But do you think you can find it with Heather? After all, although you've gone down to Devon to retire, you were born in the Home Counties, and have been a successful businessman here. So although you've never been a great man for socialising, you are, nonetheless, used to mixing with people of sophistication, education, even authority. With due respect to Heather, I hardly feel she fits into any of those categories. She's quite pretty, I'll grant you that, but . . ."

"I'll hear no more of this, Alison," snapped her father, cutting her short. He strode forward angrily onto the lawn and called loudly to his future wife still discussing the sickly azalea with Simon at the far end of the garden. "I think it's time we were off, Heather. It's a long journey home." His voice was reasonably measured in tone, but there was a touch of anger about it despite all his efforts to eliminate such an emotion.

He turned away and walked round the side of the house, closely followed by Heather and Simon, with Alison bringing up the rear. He reached the front door, then marched briskly up the path, through the open gateway, and stood by the Jag. Heather quickly unlocked the doors, turned, shook hands with Simon and Alison, and got into the driver's seat. Once he had closed the door behind her, George quickly moved forward, shook Simon by the hand and thanked him for a pleasant afternoon, then moved to his daughter standing nearby, kissed her perfunctorily upon the cheek, said, "Good-bye, Alison, and thank you for the tea," in clipped tones, got into the car, adjusted his seat belt and was whisked up the road by his chauffeuse, his half-hearted farewell wave drawing from his hosts an even more limp response.

Heather glanced at her future husband sitting beside her looking drawn and very angry. She opened her mouth to ask what was wrong, but quickly closed it again. She knew, instinctively, that Alison who had treated her with a gentle hostility throughout the entire afternoon, had obviously spoken out of turn about his future wife to her father, and had, in consequence, incurred his wrath – perhaps even his long term enmity.

It was, she decided as she steered the great white car westwards – at considerable speed – a subject best left at the moment; indeed, possibly best left for ever. The one thing she was certain of was that George's daughter, with whom her future husband had admitted he had never been as close as he would have liked, had said something – probably concerning her, and the fitness, or unfitness of her to be a wife to her father – which had widened the distance between father and daughter from gap to chasm, and it was a distance which, possibly, might never be bridged.

Chapter Seven

Heather Maunder and George Tennant plighted their troth on the second Saturday of October in the old church at Peter Tavy, before a sizeable gathering of relatives and friends – the great majority of both being on Heather's side. It pleased George, however, to note that Martin and Sylvia were there, along with Jimmy, but saddened him – though he could not honestly say it caused him surprise – that Alison and Simon had not come. They had, however, sent a present which pleased him – not for the article itself, an ornate vase, but for the thought behind it which suggested that Alison wished to, possibly, repair some of the damage she had done when they had last met in Brighton.

It proved to be a happy day, high spirits and good will abounding. The only person there who seemed a touch overwhelmed by the occasion was Arthur Maunder and such was to be expected. For on this day he had lost a daughter – or so he saw it. Granted she would almost certainly be a daily visitor to Bray Barton and, in reality, he would see almost as much of her as he had before. But it could never be the same. For whilst he got on well with, and had much pride in, his easy going son, Derek, he treasured his daughter. Ever since she was born she could do no wrong in his eyes – though, in truth, she had done little amiss in anybody's – and since the death of his wife, she had been the rock on which his life was built.

But he knew this day had to come and realised he was lucky it had not arrived before. And now that it had, he was not unaware of the fact he was fortunate he would still be seeing a great deal of his daughter, although his house would be quiet evenings and night times without her. Yet he would cope, and he knew it; he was that kind of man. But as he raised his champagne laden glass to his lips he was fully aware that a new era had dawned for all at Bray Barton and there would be no return to the old one.

The 'stars' of the day enjoyed themselves totally. For when George saw his vivacious bride standing beside him at the altar, any lingering doubts concerning the wisdom of their union – many of them revived by Alison's acerbic words – evaporated like mist around the high tors in the sun, and he could only gaze at this lovely young woman and be amazed she had chosen him as a husband and be proud that she had.

For Heather it was the day when the most elusive piece of her life's jigsaw had fallen into place. She had ever been a positive person, both giving to, and taking from life, a great deal, and had long since drawn much fulfilment from her role as a farmer's daughter – especially out of doors. For whilst she had done well at school academically, she could not wait to leave to get home to Bray Barton, work on the farm and wander the moors at will. Not that she had merely helped in recent years – she had farmed. Indeed, her knowledge of the methods and way of life of hill farming was now not far short of that of her father and, by his own admission, considerably superior to her brother's.

Also she had a greater vision, in practical terms, than either of them. So her life at Bray Barton, with her work and three horses, one or other of which she rode virtually every day up on the moor no matter what the weather, had been most fulfilling to her, as had been a full social life of the 'court all, marry none' variety. She had realised during the past couple of years though, that something was missing – some ultimate purpose for her future life. And after she had met George she became aware, rapidly, of what that was – a husband.

Not that she was in love with the idea of marriage – there was little idealistic romance within the soul of Heather Maunder. Rather, she felt that only in marriage, to the right man, could she find complete fulfilment. She had known George no more than a couple of weeks before she had realised that he was, indeed, the right man. So certain was she of this, she would have accepted him then if he had proposed to her. He had not, of course, as she knew he would not. Part of George's charm was his inherent reserve, bordering on shyness. Indeed, there was much of the traditional English gentleman about him, a factor which made Heather aware he would never propose to her unless forced, or at least cajoled – although she was confident his feelings for her were akin to hers for him; thus the bringing forward, forcibly, of the issue by her in the pub after her brother's wedding. And now on this crisp autumn day, it had all come to fruition; her life seemed now to be set upon the path which she hoped she would follow for the rest of her time on this earth.

So this day passed on its way to be followed by a honeymoon in Greece – a magical fortnight amidst warm sunshine and ancient history. They returned though, to a chill wind blowing from off the moor, the harbinger of a long winter to come. They also returned to a major problem. For they had been home barely twenty-four hours when George received a phone call from Martin. He could scarce remember a call bringing worse news.

Martin at first prevaricated a little, indulging in bland pleasantries – then plunged to the heart of the matter. "Dad, there's something I have to tell you. I knew about it when we came down for the wedding, but that was no time to talk about business – and bring bad news." At mention of the last two words, George's stomach began to churn – worry and apprehension taking a toll of his abdomen as was usual with him. For he knew what the news would be. "I'm bankrupt."

George slumped down onto the chair beside the phone, and it was some seconds – time spent by him trying to get himself together and his thoughts marshalled – before he replied. "I'm desperately sorry to hear that, Martin – for all our sakes. It's not your fault, son. It's just that everything has conspired against you; certainly you do not deserve this lot. You've worked day and night to try to make the business a success, I'm well aware of that."

"Yes – yes, that's true," agreed his son. "I've made mistakes, naturally, like everybody does, but they've not been serious ones. It's just that everything this past twelve months has been stacked against me. It's been a hellish time – I'm almost glad everything is over. At least I now know where I stand. The worst part is the problems it will cause you – having just got married and so on."

"Oh, I'll muddle through, Martin, don't worry about that. But down to brass tacks; I assume the bank have invoked my guarantee." He tried to utter the words in a matter of fact tone of voice, but suspected that the alarm which he felt manifested itself in the way he spoke to his son; this was no time to have his lifetime's savings, and more besides, taken from him to help fill

45

the vault of a fat bank.

"Yes, Dad, I'm afraid so. The amount I owe them is one hundred and forty thousand pounds – so they ensured I stopped just short of your guarantee."

"How much other debt do you have?"

"Nothing much at all. Certainly what there is will be covered by the amount owed me by the customers I deal with."

"But there's no certainty you'll get it, Martin."

"Oh, I'll get it all right; I know the companies I can trust to pay their bills. The sad thing is, though, if I could only gather in what I'm owed from some of the others, then I'd almost certainly be able to soldier on. It's those bad debts that have done for me," he concluded bitterly. "To be honest, the amount I owe apart from the bank is minimal, as I said just now. That's mainly because I tend to deal with smaller companies and, as they face the same problems as me, I attempt to pay them on time. I would rather owe money to the bank than to them."

George smiled to himself. That summed up Martin's character. He was probably too nice a man to be successful in business, he mused, before talking down the phone once more.

"It does you credit, Martin, that philosophy. Still, we've got to be practical. How long have I got before the bank will want me to settle?"

"A few months, Dad, at least. I've spoken to the manager who has always handled my business, and he's a most helpful chap. And I feel he is genuinely sorry it has come to this. But it is all way beyond his control now, of course. I suggested to him that I sell my house to raise the money, but, as he pointed out, with the way the house market is at present, it could take a very long time to sell, and even when it did go it would not produce very much. You see I've an enormous mortgage on the house, largely because I raised money for the business a couple of years back by taking out a second mortgage on it. By the time I repay all that's owing on it, there'll not be a great deal left."

"Don't you go selling your house, son," retorted his father in somewhat agitated fashion. "That's the very last thing to do. You've got Sylvia and little Jimmy to think about. Keep hold of your house whatever else you do. If you sell that now, God only knows when you will ever be able to buy another; never, I should think. So promise me you will never consider that as an option –

46

not now or ever."

"Fair enough," came the reply, spoken soothingly. "I would never have mentioned it if I had thought it would upset you in any way. It was just an option which floated through my head, along with many others. I'll not do that because I realise what you say is absolutely right. The worry for me, though, is what sort of position it will leave you in, having to pay out such an enormous sum – and how Heather will take it. Quite a shock to her it will be – and a worry I don't doubt. I am so very sorry, Dad."

"Nothing to be sorry about, Martin; it's not your fault," replied his father, truthfully. "And don't worry about Heather. I told her some weeks before we married about the problems you were having – and how my guarantee might be activated."

"And how did she take it?" The voice was pregnant with anxiety; Heather had made a sizeable impression on Martin that day they had first met, and he felt almost as guilty about burdening her with his problems as he did his father.

"As she takes everything – with a shrug of her shoulders and the simple words, 'I didn't marry you for your money'."

"Yes, I can hear her saying that; you've a good one there Dad. I'm more pleased for you than I can say. And mother would be pleased, of that I'm sure. She would not have wanted you to remain alone for the rest of your life."

"I'm sure you are right," agreed George. And he was; for prior to marrying Heather, he thought deeply of how Janet would view things if she were looking down upon him, and he came rapidly to the conclusion that she would wish him to re-marry. A practical woman, Janet had seen life as something to be lived to its fullest possibilities. The fact that she and George had always had a good marriage was no reason why, with perhaps thirty years of his life still to run, he should not seek a second fulfilling partnership – that, he was certain, would have been her philosophy.

"I hope it will not take all your savings meeting this guarantee, Dad. You worked hard for that money and I feel more upset and, to be honest, angry, than words can say that it's going to be taken from you."

"We'll get by, Martin, don't worry. And I'm sure you'll all find your feet in the future. With your ability and qualifications you'll soon get a job and then, when the time is right, you may be able to start up another business. This is but a temporary setback for you, son, of that I am sure." And he was. Martin had the tenacity and character to ensure he would not languish long in the shadow of adversity.

When the phone call ended though, after they had exchanged a few general views, and George had learnt from his son that the bank would be contacting him regarding the guarantee, he sat motionless on the hard chair in the hall next to the machine which had just brought him such catastrophic news, attempting to think things through. One hundred and forty thousand pounds – the figure rattled around his brain like a ball around a pinball machine. The brutal truth was – he did not have it. His entire savings were little more than eighty thousand pounds – thus a massive shortfall on the amount needed. He put his head down into his hands and shook it slowly from side to side. This was life playing one of its malevolent tricks, he concluded – and redressing a balance. For he had always believed good news was countered by bad. He had had the good fortune to meet and marry his lovely Heather, and his – no, their – impending impoverishment was the price which had to be paid. Not that he was too worried for himself – he had, after all, known hard times before. It was Heather who concerned him. She deserved the best – the very best of everything, and shortly he would be in a position where he was unable to give it her. Indeed – unable to give her anything.

Feeling a hand on his arm, he jerked his head from his hands, and looked up. Heather was kneeling before him. She reached out and took his hands in hers. "What is it, my darling?" she asked gently. "You look so sad – no, more than that – distressed."

He told her of Martin's call – and the dire news it brought. He shook his head, as if trying to disperse the grim news. "I really don't know how we are going to manage when the bank takes our savings," he continued, "and I've not the slightest idea as to how we shall ever raise the sixty thousand pounds shortfall."

"George, there really is no need to worry. We have all we need in material things – and more importantly, we have our love for each other which, speaking for myself, is so strong no words can adequately express it. I can face anything in life as long as I have you."

Her husband smiled at her, and nodded. "You're right – our love will carry us through. I am the most fortunate of men, Heather, for at a stage of my life when there was not that much to

48

look forward to, the future now holds so much, thanks to you – despite this very real money worry."

"That's what I wanted to hear," cooed his wife. "And regarding the sixty thousand pounds – I've got the solution."

"And it is?"

"We sell this house – simple as that."

"Sell it? But where would we live?"

"Bray Barton, of course. There's enough room there to house a regiment of soldiers. Poor old Dad's rattling around it like a single pea in a saucepan."

"True – but perhaps he likes it that way. Perhaps he wouldn't want us there."

"Wouldn't want us there? You really have to be joking, George. It would be one of the happiest days of his life if we went back there to live – and permanently. You know how close he and I have always been – and I can tell you he misses me a great deal already even though I've virtually only just ceased to live there. And he has the highest regard for you, George, so would welcome you to live under his roof."

Her husband nodded. "It could be a solution, true. This house is worth a tidy sum – though, with the market depressed, not as much as it was. Still, it has got to make two hundred thousand pounds at least. That would mean – if we got such a sum – we could pay off this dreadful guarantee and still have one hundred and forty thousand pounds odd to put by for the future. No mean sum, that." He nodded once again. "The idea appeals to me Heather, I must say – and not merely the financial side of it, either. For whilst I am quite happy living in this house, I have never put down real roots here. I've never truly thought of it as home. But Bray Barton farmhouse – that could be different. With its great age – how old is it, by the way?"

"About two hundred and fifty years."

"I thought it must be eighteenth century – it's got that look about it. With that kind of age, and its lovely setting, it possesses a character, a feeling of permanence, even tranquillity, which this house could never hope to match. Yes, I do think it would be nice to live at Bray Barton – and it would most certainly solve the financial problem. Mind you, we would have to pay our way there. Perhaps we could offer your father a lump sum and kind of buy a part of the house."

49

c

"No you couldn't," replied his wife, enigmatically.

"Why not?"

"Because he doesn't own it."

"Doesn't he? Then who does?"

"Prince Charles. The house and the farm are owned by the Duke of Cornwall – which he is, of course. The Duchy owns an enormous amount of land and property around and on Dartmoor – including Dartmoor Prison. Dad pays a yearly rental – a high one, too. A little too high for a farm so close to the moors and therefore only partially arable."

"Then we will pay rent."

"Dad'll be pleased about that. He's always on about what he has to pay the Duchy. If he can share it a bit the world will appear a far more just place to him."

"I suppose there's a reasonable security of tenure with the Duchy?" George Tennant's rather pessimistic, and somewhat cynical mind, was at work again.

"Of course there is," laughed his wife. "Why, most Duchy owned moorland farms stay in families for generations. Dad is the fourth generation Maunder, and we shall be the fifth. Mind you, there's not been one member of our family over the decades who has not longed to own the place they have farmed. But none of us have achieved it yet, and I doubt we ever will."

George smiled at his wife's unconscious allusion to him being of a younger generation than a man two years his junior, but seeing her blind spot as a compliment to himself, said nothing about it. He did, however, comment on the apparent upturn in their fortunes during the past few minutes, all down to Heather's level-headed good sense and vision.

"Heather, you've done it again," he opined, softly. "Brought sense to a confusing world, taken worry out of it, and brought happiness and peace of mind to an old man's life." He pulled his wife to him and kissed her, a gentle but lingering kiss which spoke of a heart and mind full of love for her – an embrace which was returned in full measure.

Eventually Heather stood up, smiled down at the man in her life, then moved away towards the kitchen – and the back door. "Well, I've just made one old man happy," was her departing shot. "Now I'm going to do likewise for another. I'm going to tell Dad we are coming home to live."

Chapter Eight

Heather Tennant's request of her father that she and her husband be permitted to come to Bray Barton to live was granted instantly, making the widowed farmer a happy man in the process. For whilst he had been genuinely pleased Heather had married the man she loved – and a man of whom he approved – he already missed her immensely, and only partly for the physical comfort she had long brought into his life in her role as highly efficient housekeeper. For the house and farm had always been enlivened by her energy and vivacity. And in her, Arthur Maunder saw so much of his wife, whom he still missed almost as much as he had the day she died. A fine looking woman, Jill Maunder was herself full of life and purpose, both of which were taken by a wicked cancer. Since that untimely death the farmer had been sustained through life partly by the comradeship and honest strength of his good-natured son, Derek, but mainly by Heather – his wife, as he had said to many times, not really being dead in his eyes as long as his daughter were alive.

Now she was coming home again, and vibrancy would return to the spacious, large-roomed house. It proved to be six months before the return took place, however, for with the housing market failing to sparkle, it took that time to sell George's house. They could have moved in before, of course, and left the place empty, but the estate agent advised against it: "Much easier to sell a property that is lived in," she had said, correctly.

On a chill day in late May the protracted and woefully slow process of selling a house was brought to a satisfying conclusion as far as George and Heather were concerned, when their joint account was swollen by a cheque for around one hundred and eighty thousand pounds, and a youngish couple with two children

– again, from London – moved into their former abode. The newly married couple were pleased with the sale, for lengthy business though it was, it had still taken place quicker than the estate agent had forecast – "the market gets slower by the day" – and at a higher price than they had dared to hope for. The estate agent had suggested they put the property on at a figure under two hundred thousand pounds, but on the theory it was always easier to come down in price than to go up, they insisted it be advertised for two hundred and twenty thousand and were delighted that within a reasonable time of the house being put up for sale, they received an offer of over two hundred thousand pounds.

The excessive demands of estate agent, solicitor and Inland Revenue accounted for more than twenty thousand pounds, unfortunately, but the cheque they eventually received was as respectable as it was welcome. So the bank guarantee regarding Martin's debt was met in full, and a sizeable sum remained to be invested for the future – whatever that might bring. Martin was deeply grateful to his father for his remarkable financial generosity, and came down one weekend with Sylvia and Jimmy to tell him. He also told his young stepmother how much he appreciated all that she had done when informed by George that it was Heather's suggestion the house be sold to pay off his debt.

"You're a lucky man, Dad, having such a wonderful wife," he had said to his father with total sincerity – though out of the hearing of his Sylvia who might have misunderstood such a statement. If only, mused George, his daughter Alison felt the same way about Heather. But then he had expected her to react in much that way. It saddened him still, however, that there was a rift between himself and his daughter, the sole communication between them since his wedding being an exchange of Christmas cards. He hoped one day there would be a reconciliation, but had not the least idea as to how it would be brought about.

The months which followed saw George Tennant really begin to get some sort of grip on 'this farming lark', as he often called it. Yet though he would use the phrase to lighten a conversation, he became fully aware of what he had long-suspected – that farming, most assuredly was no 'lark'. The opposite, in fact; it was possibly the most professional occupation in existence, and amongst the most difficult to master if you were not born to it. This was made apparent to him one day in July when he went out with Arthur after breakfast one morning to see if a field of hay was ready to bale. On reaching the large enclosure, they alighted from the Land Rover and strolled to the middle of the mown meadow. Arthur then bent down picked up a handful of the dry, yellow grass, and raised it to his nose, George doing likewise.

"Feels dry," opined the apprentice farmer. "Ready to bale I would think, Arthur – isn't it?" The final words were said without conviction.

"Not yet, George. It needs a few more hours sun on its back. Too sappy at present."

"Doesn't look like we're going to get much sun today," said George, looking up at the overcast sky. "In fact, it looks like it could rain."

Arthur shook his head. "There's no rain about, boy. Too hazy for that. It's only high cloud; the sun'll be up before noon. Should be ready to bale about three o'clock."

"How do you know all that," asked a puzzled son-in-law.

"Because I've been at this game all my life, and my father, grandfather and great-grandfather before me – and always on Bray Barton. It's in my blood George; I'm afraid it can never be in yours. But that doesn't mean you won't make a farmer one day; you will. And before too long, as well; that's because you're willing to learn and listen. You'll never have the instinct for it, mind you, such as a man like me has got and young Derek for that matter – but you will gain enough practical knowledge, and be willing to heed enough of us old hands, to keep you out of the bankruptcy court. And, mark you, you've an advantage over most townies who come into the farming business – you're married to a woman who knows it inside out. She doesn't know as much as I do yet mind, but she will before long."

The relevance and wisdom of Arthur Maunder's prediction became apparent to him later that day when several hundred bales of perfectly dry hay were made in this field under a blazing summer sun.

Arthur's words did not fall on stony ground as far as his son-in-law was concerned. From then on there was no job about the farm which he did not attempt to do. Not that he had shirked any in the past, but now he sought out the tasks which he had never before done and worked at them until he was tolerably efficient, if not adept.

Also he spent much of his time asking questions and absorbing answers. And there was nobody whose mind he picked more than that of his wife, finding out in the process that her father's words were correct – there appeared to be nothing about livestock and the land that Heather did not know.

The principal reason why he wished to learn, naturally, was to make himself more proficient in tackling the myriad tasks which came his way during the average working week. But also, now that he was on the payroll at Bray Barton, he felt obliged to perform his work to an acceptable standard even though the highest levels of skill might be, and remain, beyond him.

So the farming year wended its slow but inexorable course with many tasks performed daily, others coming and going with the seasons. Haymaking inter-mingled with sheep shearing and dipping – a major task when there was such a mighty flock to be attended to – then came the buying and transporting of straw from the lowland farms south of Tavistock, to act as bedding for stock during the winter, a hill farm such as Bray Barton being too cold and wet for the growing of corn, even if the thin soil would produce a crop.

Then the autumn, with the major sheep and livestock sales traditionally beginning and ending with the two ancient, and massive markets at Tavistock – St. John's Fair (known locally as Jan's Fair) in September, and Goose Fair in October – with numerous others in various places in between. Here were sold the lambs from the spring crop, and the ewes whose productive life was over, whilst bought in would be younger potential mothers to take their place.

George attended many of these sales – along with Heather, Arthur and on occasions Derek – finding the atmosphere intoxicating, even exhilarating. For here was Devon as he always had imagined it; gnarled farmers from off the moor rubbing shoulders with their more affluent looking cousins from the lowland farms – though appearances often deceived when it came to relative wealth – the smartly dressed dealers from all over the county, indeed the country, the occasional gypsy, farm representatives in thick trousers and heavy shoes trying to espy some of their regular customers, local townsfolk strolling around viewing all that was taking place, young jean clad boys and girls taking, often, an illicit day off school, indeed, all sections of the diverse

54

groups which make a rural community where large numbers of people are dependent, directly or indirectly, upon the land for their living. But although the apprentice farmer soaked up the atmosphere eagerly, and quietly cursed himself for so rarely having visited any of these fairs during the six or so years he had lived in Devon, he realised that there were more important aspects to these colourful days than merely absorbing the atmosphere. The purpose of the fairs was quite simply to buy and sell sheep, beef and store cattle, and that process was a skill all of its own.

George watched, almost in awe, as Arthur picked out the pens of breeding ewes he wished to purchase, taking note of their quality and the number of teeth they possessed – the making of mother's milk to succour young lambs was dependent on the ewe eating sufficient fodder, and the creature could not do that if she did not have good and plentiful teeth – their general condition and age, whilst making a mental note of the sum he was willing to go to in buying them.

On the selling side, Arthur fixed in his own mind the amount he required for a pen of lambs and would rarely let them go for less. Likewise, the 'townie' took note of the farmer's judgement in buying and selling the beef and store cattle, an even more difficult task than with the sheep, simply because the value of cattle – and thus the scope to make a loss in a bad deal – was so much higher.

Heather was perpetually delighted with the efforts which her husband took to assimilate himself into the rather exclusive, perceptive, knowledgeable – though in many ways reactionary – ranks of Devonshire hill farmers, and even more delighted that his efforts were bearing fruit. For within a year or so of their marriage, George, with her help, would have been able to run Bray Barton in the short term if, for any reason, her father and Derek were absent. And not only did she realise it, but he did also – which gave him a confidence he never thought could be his when it came to this farming business.

So the second Christmas of their marriage saw George Tennant feeling some modest personal esteem – something he had not truly known since his retirement from business – with his young wife gaining pleasure and pride from her husband's tenacious efforts to build a fulfilling life for them both. And these positive movements towards fulfilment manifested themselves in yuletide celebrations as good and enjoyable as any of them had known for years. "The best Christmas I've known since your mother died," as Arthur Maunder said to his daughter.

There were five of them at Bray Barton for Christmas dinner – three permanent residents, plus Derek and Elaine. And a superb meal, prepared and cooked by Heather, was brought to a most successful conclusion when Elaine announced she was expecting a baby the early part of the following July. All were delighted, naturally, but none more so than Arthur. For like so many men of the land, the farmer felt keenly the importance of heredity. He had taken over Bray Barton from his father, who in turn had succeeded Grandfather Maunder, and so on. Likewise, when he died, Derek, nominally, would be boss at Bray Barton, being the male of the line, although Heather would, in reality, be a partner as she was now. And with this news, he knew that when Derek passed on, his son – the possibility of Elaine giving birth to a girl never entered the farmer's head – would be master of Bray Barton. With that in mind, Arthur rose from his seat at the head of the dinner table, stood erect, though a mite unsteady on his feet – he had not stinted on the wine during the meal – raised his glass, and bellowed, "A toast to the next Maunder – may he be here with us, fit and well, when we sit down at this table next Christmas Day."

"Or she," added Heather, quickly, aware the odds were even it could be a little girl in the crib next Christmas.

Glasses were raised, wine was drunk, and good fellowship permeated the warm air of the huge dining-room, which was rarely used more than two or three times a year, Christmas Day being the sole hardy annual.

The next occasion when the dining-room was put to use was Easter Sunday, a wild stormy day at the end of March. The numbers at the table were swollen that day, the five who had partaken of Christmas dinner being joined by Martin, Sylvia and Jimmy who had accepted a long standing invitation from George and Heather to come down and spend a few days with them. It was another happy day because Martin had at last put the traumas of his bankruptcy behind him, and had secured a managerial job with a large company no more than five miles from his home. "It's coming right for us at last, Dad," he had told his father the previous evening. "It's a good job, has got excellent prospects and it's well paid. And talking of money, when we get back on our feet, Sylvia and I – which hopefully should not be too long – then I'm going to start paying back some of the money I owe you."

"You owe me nothing," his father had replied – but Martin was adamant.

"Dad, I owe you everything, including my sanity; it was all worrying me into a mental home; and – it's an old fashioned word to use, I know – but I owe you my honour. I'll never forget what you did for me – for us – and the sum is so large I doubt I'll ever be able to pay it all back. But I will make the effort to pay you what I can afford. And I'm sure the money will be handy to you, Dad. After all, you're a married man now, and have a wife to support," he concluded, grinning broadly.

His father had smiled and nodded by way of reply; actually, there was news he had to impart on the question of whom he had to support, but that would keep just a little while longer.

The Easter feast had been devoured, and generous quantities of wine and beer imbibed, especially by Derek – though little by George. He was not permitted to drink with the medication he was taking daily, and probably would not have even if it were not forbidden him. For he was going to take no risks now. He had gone almost eighteen months without an attack; thus, if he went another half year free from a fainting fit, then he could apply for the return of his driving licence; and the gaining of that priceless document would return a dimension to his life the value of which he had not appreciated until it had been taken from him.

The dinner finished, Arthur and Derek lit cigars as they did, invariably, upon occasions such as these, and persuaded Martin to join them. Then, after a few puffs on his pungent, magnificent looking rolled leaf, Arthur proceeded to regale the assembly with a few of his old farming tales, all of them true – according to him. Derek and Heather had heard most before, and George a few. Martin and Sylvia though, were fresh, fertile soil for them, and rolled around in mirth at the tales which invariably involved a wily Devonshire farmer and a townie still wet behind the ears. Arthur was an excellent story-teller, and his son and daughter still enjoyed hearing the tales even though they knew many virtually word for word. After about half an hour non-stop talking, however, the rich food and abundant drink seemed to catch up with the farmer – and he lapsed into a contented silence.

As nobody else seemed in any hurry to tell their own tales, not a word was spoken for what seemed an age, though in reality, it was only about twenty seconds. The silence, however, was broken by Heather who took an almost imperceptible nod from her husband as the pre-arranged signal for her to impart news known only to themselves. "Now we are all here together," she said softly, almost shyly, "there's something George and I want you to know. The fact is, Dad is going to be a grandfather twice this year; I am going to have a baby in October. She turned in her seat and looked at her husband sitting beside her – a look of utter and total love the like of which George had never before known – and grasped his right hand. "We are so happy about it," she commented simply, but more than adequately.

"And so are we, maid – so are we," cried Arthur Maunder, his face ablaze with delight. "What a year this is; I'm going to be a grandfather twice – as you said just now Heather. I can scarce believe it all. But I tell you this – it's a long time since I've felt as happy as I do now. If only your mother were here to share it all, Heather – Derek," he added quickly, anxious to include his son in his feelings of supreme satisfaction and fulfilment. For he would do or say nothing to hurt his son in any way – their relationship was far too close to allow that. Indeed, special though Arthur and Heather's understanding had always been – with that iron like bond that so often exists between father and daughter – the farmer's bond with his son had been as close in its own way. Derek and he were of similar nature and outlook, phlegmatic, essentially easy going men, but resilient and strong minded nonetheless – men born to the soil who would never find true satisfaction anywhere else. Indeed, their relationship was more that of brothers rather than father and son, although Arthur made all the major decisions regarding the farm, Derek never questioning them.

The farmer arose from his seat, and went to the drinks cabinet on the far side of the room. He rummaged in it for half a minute or so, then pulled out a large bottle of champagne. "I was sure there was one here," he chirped, happily, holding the bottle aloft. "We had one at Christmas when Derek and Elaine gave us their good news, so we'll have the other now in honour of Heather and

George."

Elaine and Derek fetched glasses, and within seconds they were filled, clasped in hands and raised towards the ceiling in celebration of the latest pair of expectant parents at Bray Barton, goodwill and happiness dancing in the air like the bubbles from the glasses.

One amongst the revellers, though, was less happy than he should have been, or thought he would be. George Tennant went through the motions of showing delight concerning his wife's pregnancy, but he felt it not. Rather he was seized by cold, gnawing apprehension. Strangely, when he married Heather he never thought of how he would feel if they were blessed with children. Now he was not sure his wife's pregnancy was a blessing. When he had contemplated marriage to a wife less than half his age, the gap between them of some twenty-six years had concerned him greatly; those doubts, though, had largely evaporated before the warmth of their mutual love. Now, however, all those worries had returned. After all, he mused, if the age gap between Heather and himself was cause for concern, the age gulf between himself and a baby son or daughter would be enormous. Indeed, he could well be dead long before the child had grown to adulthood, thereby leaving Heather to be both mother and father – and help run the farm as well.

And, he had to admit, there was an element of selfishness involved. For he had rarely known happiness and contentment to match that which had become his during eighteen months of marriage to this farmer's daughter. Now it would all change, inevitably. He would no longer be the sole recipient of the abundance of love which Heather had within her. Soon, he would have to share her with a child, and he was not at all sure he would find it easy to come to terms with. And there was the practical side of the matter. Getting out in the middle of the night to comfort a crying child was something he thought he had left behind for good a quarter century before. But he faced it all once again – that, and the myriad problems, illnesses, anxieties that are the lot of parents with young children – and he did not welcome the thought of it at all. Life, he found, was full and exacting enough with him trying to master the elusive craft of farming in the foothills of Dartmoor, without the added

59

responsibility of a vulnerable and highly demanding baby.

So as he toasted his wife and himself in the excellent champagne which his father-in-law had provided, George Tennant's mood was alien to the high tide of joy and hope with which Bray Barton appeared to be awash.

Chapter Nine

George Tennant had never been good at hiding his feelings, try though he may. Add that to the fact that Heather was a most perceptive woman and it became a certainty she would soon realise her husband was worried, or depressed about something. And as she had become aware that this melancholy had settled upon him since she had told him of her pregnancy, she was quite certain – with a measure of alarm – that the forthcoming child was the cause of his depression. Never a person to turn a blind eye to problems, or to delay the tackling of them, she brought up the subject less than a week after her Easter Sunday announcement.

George had just come in from the large garden at the back of the house as dusk began to fall on a quite mild, but cloudy early April evening. He washed his hands at the kitchen sink, then filled the electric kettle and put it on to boil – a great man for his tea, was George. "Been busy," asked his wife, sitting beside the large modern Aga cooker performing her now regular evening task of knitting baby clothes.

"Yes," he replied, coming across to sit opposite her, keen to get the weight off his tired legs whilst the kettle boiled. "I put in a few spuds. I wasn't sure whether to or not, but thought I might as well have a go. After all, the soil's nice and damp and the weather's mild; they should grow all right."

"I would think so – good growing weather at present. And the quicker they grow the sooner we can eat them. I love new potatoes – and they'll build me up for what's in store," she added, tapping her tummy as she spoke. He smiled wanly, and looked away, a desperate feeling of guilt within him. Heather got up from her chair, walked around to where he sat, then perched herself on the arm of the chair. She took his hands in her. "What's troubling you, George," she asked, gently, her face full of concern – with a touch of sadness about it. "These days should be so happy for us both. They certainly are for me but you look so forlorn I almost feel guilty the way I am – so glad to be alive, so full of hope and happiness. What is it, my darling; please tell me."

"Nothing, Heather; nothing at all. I just get a bit tired that's all. Bound to, though, aren't I. After all, I'm an old man."

"Stuff and nonsense, George," she retorted, sharply. "You're not old, for heaven's sake – as I've told you so many times before. You must not think so often of the past, something I notice you doing increasingly; you must think of the future and all the good, positive things it holds in store. You must think of our baby George – and how he, or she, will make our life together even better; even more complete." She stopped talking as he looked away from her, but soon found her voice again.

"That's it, George, isn't it – the baby. It occurred to me just a couple of days ago that your depression came upon you when I told you I was pregnant. That is the problem, George, isn't it? The baby, I mean?" Her voice was soft, as it usually was, but insistent. She asked a question which he knew he had to answer.

He shook his head. "No – no, it's nothing to do with the baby. It's just I'm a bit down at present, Heather, that's all. You must remember that all this farming business is new to me still, and I find it very hard work – both physically and mentally. It's different for your dad – and for Derek; they were weaned on this way of life. But I came to it very late and find it all very much a new world to me. Not that I'm complaining, mind you, I'm not. Basically I find it all a worthwhile challenge – perhaps even an enjoyable one – but it does, at times, get on top of me."

He spoke the words without looking his wife in the eye. Not that they were untrue. He often asked himself when taking fodder up onto the windswept, sodden moor to feed the stock, or viewed his cold, chapped hands after a spell of stone hedging, or was bowled over by some bad-tempered ram, what exactly he, a townie, who had known nothing of rural England – other than what he gleaned from driving through it – for virtually half a century, was doing putting himself through this kind of hell at his age. It was true, of course, that when he occasionally sat in the front garden of Bray Barton farmhouse on, say, a sunny afternoon with his beloved wife close by him, any doubts he might have had over his still relatively new way of life evaporated – but that did not mean to say they did not exist.

Heather, however, though aware that what he had just said to her expressed the way he often felt, knew also that most of the time, despite its hardships, he gleaned much satisfaction from his new found role as an 'apprentice' hill farmer. She was also well aware, in her intuitive way, that what he had just told her was not the main reason for his depression.

"It's the baby George," she reiterated. "That's the cause of you being so down. You're worried about becoming a father because you think you are too old. Am I not right?" Her voice was now uncharacteristically sharp in tone, and had an edge to it which suggested she would accept nothing but the truth from him – and would be aware if he failed to tell it.

He turned his head so that he looked directly into her eyes. He knew he had to tell her exactly how he felt; he owed her total truth because he knew well enough by now that she could cope with honest words no matter how painful they might be – but would be decimated if the man she loved resorted to telling her lies.

He nodded in agreement. "Yes, sweetheart, it's the baby. And as you say, I worry about having a young child because of my age. Let's face it, I'll be an old man – a really old man – well into pension – before he or she even leaves school. I could even be dead; that's put brutally, but it's the truth none-the-less. But it's more than that my love – I'm ashamed to say." He ceased his confessions momentarily, pulled the soiled handkerchief from his pocket and dabbed at the tears welling in his eyes. "I'm sorry Heather – I'm sorry I've got myself into such a state. I'm like a child myself."

"A very loving child," murmured his wife, leaning forward and kissing him gently on the lips.

He looked at her for several seconds, choked with emotion. He shook his head, almost violently. He did not deserve her and felt like saying it. But no, he would not. For if he did, she would only say kind and loving words to him and he most assuredly did not deserve that. He deserved few good things from life the way he had behaved since his wife had told him of the baby.

He dropped his head into his hands and began to weep, the handkerchief, still clasped in his left hand, only partially stemming the flow of tears. Heather put her arms about him as if he were a small child, and gently cooed.

"George, my darling, what is it? Why are you so upset? Tell me – do please tell me."

And he did, the words pouring from his lips like water from a fountain. "I feel so ashamed, Heather – so disgusted with myself. I don't deserve to be a father again – and I certainly don't deserve you as a wife. You see, it's more than just that I feel I am too old to be the father of a baby; the main reason if I'm honest with myself, is that I am jealous. The fact is, I love you more than any words can say. Not that I love you any more than I loved Janet – I don't. She and I shared a deep and, I feel, mutually satisfying love for each other. We had a truly wonderful marriage. Yet it was different than my marriage to you – if for no other reason that I was much younger then, and we were of a similar age, Janet and I. You see, when you are a young man you take love, marriage and children all in your stride; it is the natural progression of life, after all – milestones. But when you get into middle age, and lose your wife – with your children grown up – you expect nothing more from the world in terms of love and romance. At least, I didn't. Then along you came, and my life was no longer my own – and still isn't, and probably never will be again. Even now, though we have been married more than eighteen months, I can still scarce believe it – a woman as beautiful as you, who could have had her pick of all the most eligible young men in the area, loving and marrying somebody like me, a man twice your age, with the best years of my life behind me. But I know it's not a dream; we are married and you have made my life so happy again.

"And now, you're going to have a baby and – and I'm terrified he or she will come between us; that the love you have given me – so much – will be given to the baby instead, and I'll be left out in the cold. I couldn't stand that, Heather. But then, I'm selfish, I'm only too well aware of that. More than that, I do not deserve to have you as my wife. I can never truly tell you just how ashamed I feel; in fact, just how disgusted I am with myself. But you wanted me to tell you, so I have. The one thing you can be sure of is that I will always tell you the truth."

Heather kissed him again, then took the handkerchief from his hand and wiped away the tears which clustered about his eyes like dewdrops. "Oh George," she said in a voice little more than a whisper, "you really have worked yourself up, haven't you – and all for nothing. After all, I'm sure just about every man in your position would feel the same as you do now – and with some cause. For you are at a time of life when babies being born into your family are usually grandchildren, not your own. And having had years of sleepless nights and worrying about your kids, you expect it all to be over when they grow up. You certainly do not expect to get into your fifties and start all over again. Yet our son or daughter – although I've a feeling it will be a son – will bring so much joy to our lives, darling; as much to yours as to mine. He will keep you young – and give you a purpose in life."

"You give me a purpose in life."

"Yes, I know that. But a little child, the product of our great love for each other will increase it. In fact, it will bring a new dimension to both our lives. We will be totally fulfilled, darling, and our lives will be even better than now. For our love for each other will be bonded – bonded forever – through our love for our child. And you will love him – or her," she added, with a smile. "You will love our baby as much as you love me, of that I am certain." She leant forward again and kissed him with some passion this time, then rested back against her chair. "Am I not right, George?"

He nodded, then smiled, and suddenly he looked years younger, the aspect of melancholy having deserted him for the first time in weeks. His face regained its natural expression of affability, and his relative good looks seemed to return in place of the tight, pinched expression which had clouded them.

"Yes, you are right, my love," he replied. "In fact, you are usually right about everything. I don't know what took hold of me. How stupid I've been – and selfish. And I don't know why I didn't talk to you concerning it before. All the doubts, the worries – the jealousies – have suddenly gone. I can scarce believe they ever existed. And I don't know what they were all about now. After all, I'm not too old to be a father, am I? In fact, with my experience of having brought up two already, I reckon I am the perfect age."

His wife's gentle but perceptive talk to him that evening had done even more for George Tennant than he had realised at the time. For it had seemingly given him a new lease of life, and not only in terms of him now looking forward to the birth of the baby. For on the farm, so much of his previous doubt and despondency had left him and he approached it all with a positive enthusiasm which made it easier for him to absorb the myriad range of knowledge which a farmer needed if his livestock was to be brought, and kept, to the necessary standard and his land was to be farmed to profit.

The spring was dry and warm, too much so for an area accustomed to rain, and needing it regularly. There was, though, sufficient precipitation to produce enough grass for a reasonable hay harvest, and the hot July sun ensured there was no trouble drying it and bringing it into the Dutch barn. It was at the midst of the hay harvest that Elaine was delivered of a fine baby girl, much to the delight of all at Bray Barton – although Arthur and Derek had hoped for a boy so that the 'family name' could be carried forward at least another generation. This, however, in no way inhibited the 'wetting of the baby's head' celebrations which were held in the local pub a couple of days after her birth; during the long session, Derek told the gathered throng his daughter was to be christened Louise Elaine and proceeded to get so comprehensively drunk that when 'time' was called, he had to be carried from the pub and lain in the back of his brother-in-law's Jaguar. The motor was driven by Heather who had spent the evening avoiding alcohol – partly due to her duties as chauffeuse, but also because there were minor problems with her pregnancy and her doctor had advised against the imbibing of any alcohol. George was also stone cold sober because of a like doctor's ban on drink, but still not permitted to drive – a situation he hoped would be rectified the following October. As for Arthur, he became almost as inebriated as his son, but remained on his legs although they looked as if they would give out on him at any moment.

As was ever the case with over indulgence, the following morning told the tale. Derek looked like a walking corpse whilst Arthur spent a goodly portion of the morning laying on the settee in the sitting-room. What outdoor tasks that were performed were done by George who drove a battered old tractor, attached to an almost new hay turner, up and down a field of grass close to the farmhouse which had been mown only the previous day, able to remain within the law, despite his lack of licence, as he did not have to drive on a public road.

He spent most of the morning guiding the tractor around the field, the bulky turner battering the life – and what little sap the broiling summer sun had not eliminated – out of the rapidly yellowing grass. It was fortunate the field would not be ready to bale that day, he mused, the dust swirling about him, for had it been then he would have ended up trying to do it all himself – an impossible task – his partners and colleagues in no fit state to tackle anything more than glasses of Alka Seltzer. The grass was drying by the minute, though, and would certainly bale the following day if the sun remained as fierce as it was at present. It was assuredly July at its most stifling – thus, the year at its hottest. He remembered hot, sunny days in London with his printing workshop seemingly as hot as an Arab bazaar, plus a polluted heat haze hanging over the vast city. They had been good days, he mused; these, though, were better – here amidst the rolling swath of rural Devon, with the grandeur of Dartmoor rising starkly, but majestically, above him, and his beautiful young wife, pregnant with his child, no more than a quarter mile away.

The grass turned, and re-turned, he headed his tractor towards the gate on the far side of the field, beyond which lay the farmyard and house. Half past one, he noted, glancing at his watch – not too bad at all. He would be able to have a reasonably leisurely lunch before going out to check the steers which were cropping the dry, spiky grass in the field at the far end of the farm, bordering the moor. With the drought, and the heat, the brown beasts were more vulnerable than normal to all manner of diseases and sickness, so needed checking at least once, and preferably twice, each day. Heather had prepared a refreshing salad for lunch, and having eaten it, George sat down in an easy chair on the far side of the kitchen to have a nap – a custom of his when the weather was hot and tiring. It was, however, to be a brief one. For no sooner had his eyes closed, than Derek's voice, seemingly still slurred from the previous evenings jollifications, forced them open again.

"Will you tell Dad, George, that there's hardly any water running out there in the Brook Field where the steers are. There's definitely not enough to keep those bullocks going in this hot weather and the stream's the only source of water out that way as you know. Lucky I came that way. I hadn't intended to 'cause I knew you were going out to check them this afternoon. But I couldn't find a couple of the yearlings which were supposed to be in Tree Meadow, and thought they might somehow have got out there with the steers. As it is I'm told they've somehow got across the road into Jack Craddock's place. I saw Jack's missus, Sally, just now as she walked past the yard gate on her way to the village and she told me they're there. He's got 'em penned up in his yard, and she said if I go right over, he'll help me bring 'em back."

"Shall I come with you?"

"No – I can manage. You best tell Dad, and the both of you go up on the moor and see what's happened to that stream. It can't have dried up – that's never happened in living memory. Somebody's diverted it further up, I reckon. Not the first time it's happened. Well, I'm over to Jack Craddock's to bring back those yearlings."

With that, the farmer's son had staggered wearily out into the sunshine, leaving his brother-in-law to get to his feet, stretch, and await Arthur Maunder whom Heather, hearing her brother's conversation, had gone to awaken. The farmer came into the kitchen, his face as pallid as whitewash despite the heat of the sun. "Problems with the water out in the Brook Field, Derek says. It looks as if . . ."

"Yes, I know – Heather's just told me," replied the farmer, his voice little more than a whisper. He did not look at all well. "We'll have to go up above the field to the moor. Some useless lout's put some boulders in the stream up there and has either dammed it or diverted it. We had something similar happen a couple of years back – didn't we Heather? And that wasn't the first time either."

His daughter nodded. "Yes, I remember that well. Someone had put a huge boulder in the stream and had diverted it into another gully leading nowhere. That's what's happened this time, you may depend. It'll probably be a two man job to move it, though, so you had both best go." The two men nodded agreement and ambled out into the sultry air, after George had kissed his, by now, noticeably pregnant wife, good-bye. They clambered aboard the Land Rover and headed up a rutted lane which led directly onto the moor.

"One thing about it, we can drive right up to the spot where the obstruction probably lies," opined the farmer, pulling an old trilby hat he was in the habit of wearing in sunny weather, down over his eyes to shield them from glare.

They followed the meandering track until it broke onto the open moorland, then cut across, diagonally upwards towards a tor whose craggy rocks dominated the skyline. Below them lay Brook Field with the cattle laying peacefully in what little shade they could find, their tails swishing to and fro' like snaking pendulums as they attempted, with no great measure of success, to keep away the flies. Despite his hung-over state, Arthur guided the Land Rover adroitly between and around the multitude of boulders which littered the rough terrain, aiming all the time for the stream which snaked down through the moor towards Bray Barton's furthermost fields, below them. At last they were beside the stream which carried now a trickle so slight it was in danger of drying up completely in the unrelenting sun. Arthur began to drive, slowly, straight up the tor, the dying stream to the right, his guide. Suddenly his left arm shot out pointing directly ahead of them. "There it is – exactly where it happened the last time. See that big boulder? Well, that's what's causing the trouble," continued the farmer without waiting for an answer.

He brought the sturdy Land Rover to a halt some ten yards from the source of their problems, scrambled out, and walked over to where a large rock lay blocking the natural path of the stream, causing a surprisingly abundant amount of water, considering the protracted dry spell, to be diverted into a wide gully which carried it down across the moor to nowhere in particular.

"Well, George, it's straightforward enough; we've got to get the blasted thing moved. Not the best of jobs on a day such as this."

Nor was it. Yet, working together under Arthur's instructions, they had, within about ten minutes of heavy toil, succeeded in getting the offending stone 'dam' out of the bed of the stream and up onto the bank some three feet above. Having got it there, they rested for a few seconds before pushing it down the hill where it came to rest some fifteen yards away against a cluster of slab-like rocks.

Arthur pulled a handkerchief from a trouser pocket, mopped his brow, and noticed, with satisfaction, the healthy amount of water now bubbling down the stream towards Bray Barton away below them.

"Well, that problem's solved, George. I don't know what comedian did this, but I'd like to lay hold of him, I know that."

"Yes, I'm with you there, Arthur; but I doubt we'll ever find out who did it. Some malicious louts who take pleasure only from causing harm to others, I reckon."

"Not necessarily boy," said the farmer, still mopping his sweat laden brow. "A lot of these things are done by people who look upon the moor as some kind of playground. They don't know what sort of place it really is – how a simple stupid act can cause harm, even death, to animals – and sometimes people. They would probably have diverted that stream just for the hell of it; I doubt they realised it would put a bunch of steers in danger of dehydrating. Still," he added, shrugging his shoulders, "I reckon we've better things to do than stand here moralising. Let's get back down to the house and have a cup of tea."

He began to walk down the gentle incline towards the Land Rover nearby, his son-in-law following a couple of paces behind. Skirting a mighty boulder, he stopped suddenly, appeared to stiffen to the point of rigidity, then pitched forward, fortunately falling onto a patch of spongy, grass-ridden peat. George stood for a few seconds gazing at him before the reality of what had happened seized him. Then he bounded forward and turned the sturdy farmer onto his back. He noted the uneven breathing, the face awash with sweat – far more than even a hot day such as this should create – and convinced himself that Arthur had suffered a heart attack.

He remembered a fellow who had worked for him in his London printing works dropping in such an alarming way and looking similar. That had been heart trouble and his life had been saved due to the prompt arrival of an ambulance and his speedy removal to hospital. That, though, had been London; this was Dartmoor, with miles of winding tracks and lanes lying between them and anywhere and everywhere. For sure, the only hope of the farmer surviving what appeared a major attack – and layman though he was, George Tennant was certain that was what his father-in-law had suffered – was to get him to Tavistock hospital as soon as possible. And it was no use sending for an ambulance; by the time one came out from Tavistock, collected the patient and made it back to the hospital Arthur could well be dead. Chillingly, he was certain, on this hot day, that Arthur Maunder's only hope of continued life lay in his hands – down to the speed with which he could get this good man to the hospital.

Rapidly he thrust his hands under the farmer's shoulders, slipped them into his armpits, lifted his back and head slightly off the ground, and hauled him slowly but determinedly down the remaining few yards to the back of the Land Rover. He lay the sick man on the ground, flipped down the low tail board, then, straining himself to the very limit, succeeded in lifting the heavy fellow into the back, laying him on the floor of the vehicle, supporting his head with an old piece of sacking which he found under the driver's seat.

Breathlessly, he clambered into that seat, started the engine and drove the sturdy 'workhorse' of the farm as fast as he dared down across the treacherous moor. After what seemed an eternity, the Land Rover arrived at the mouth of the rocky lane which led down to the farmhouse. George stepped up the speed a little – even though the lane was most uneven – for he knew that if Arthur's trouble was his heart, then every minute counted. He would get down to the house he mused, call Heather and get her to drive the patient and himself into Tavistock hospital in the Jag; it was assuredly doing his father-in-law no good being ferried in the sturdy, but bone shaking Land Rover.

He glanced briefly away from the lane down into the yard at the back of the house, which he could see clearly – and was immediately overwhelmed with despair. For where the Jag was normally parked, and Derek's Escort, there was but space. Sudden remembrance came to him; Heather had gone into town shopping – she had told him of her intention at lunch and Derek had gone around to Jack Craddock's to bring home the wandering yearlings.

As the yard drew ever nearer he realised he had to make a decision so crucial it frightened him; he had to decide whether he should phone for an ambulance, and take a chance as to whether or not it would arrive in time to save the life of the fellow who lay stricken in the back of the Land Rover, or whether he should ignore the vital fact he had no driving licence, or insurance and drive Arthur straight to hospital himself.

As he entered the yard, he made his decision, and transmitted it to a right foot which pushed down on the accelerator. He saw no reason, other than a malevolent fate, why he should be stopped by the police during his five mile journey to Tavistock, but even if he was, at least they would ensure Arthur was rushed to hospital as quickly as was humanly possible.

He glanced over his shoulder at the sick man, saw the ghastly pallor of his face, heard the gasping breathing and made up his mind that no matter what laws he had to break, Arthur Maunder would travel to Tavistock quicker than he had possibly done in his entire life. And George Tennant almost certainly achieved it. He hurtled, often dangerously, through the narrow lanes until he hit the main road, then pushed the accelerator pedal down to the boards as he thundered towards Tavistock, then through it, to the hospital situated on the far side of town. And strangely, he felt so confident in his driving it was as if the gap of almost two years since he had last driven on public roads, had never existed.

He roared into the hospital forecourt, then right up to the main doors. Slamming on the hand brake and turning off the ignition both at the same time, he looked over his shoulder at his passenger, saw him still breathing, then jumped out and rushed into the Victorian building, praying as he went that there was a doctor on duty. For this was a small hospital with no resident doctors; rather, the local GPs took it in turns to administer to the patients. He was no sooner inside the building, though, than his prayers were answered; for he saw the imposing figure of Doctor Conway standing further down the corridor, apparently studying an X-ray.

"Why — George, whatever's the matter?" He had recently started calling his patient by his Christian name, for he had spent quite a bit of time at Bray Barton during the past few weeks — being Heather's doctor as well as his, he had been keeping a strict eye on her during what was proving an exacting, if not fraught pregnancy.

The rookie farmer hastily explained the situation and Conway flew into action with a speed which was almost startling in such a big, and by no means young man. Telling George to go into the waiting room, get a cup of tea from the machine and rest himself as best he could, the doctor appeared to conjure a nurse, an orderly and a stretcher from thin air, and they hastily went about their business.

George obtained an ill tasting cup of tea lying uninvitingly in a cardboard beaker, from the machine, and sat down to await news of his father-in-law, and had few doubts it would be a long time coming. In that, though, he was wrong, for he had not long finished his beverage when Doctor Conway entered the reasonably comfortable waiting room, his rather lethargic demeanour and lugubrious expression suggesting to the son-in-law that all was not well with his beloved wife's father. George got to his feet swiftly upon the doctor's entry and moved forward to confront him.

"What's happening, doctor? How's Arthur?" he asked the questions in hope, but a glance at Conway's face was sufficient to dash it.

The doctor shook his head. "Very bad news, George, I'm afraid; the worst, in fact; Arthur's dead. He was dead when we fetched him from the Land Rover."

"Surely not," cried George. "I mean, I glanced at him just before I ran in here to get help, and I could swear he was still breathing."

"No, I'm afraid not," replied the doctor. "You probably thought he was because you wanted him to be – the mind can play tricks in times such as these. No, I fancy he was dead five to ten minutes before he reached here. We'll know better after the post-mortem, of course, but my feeling is that it will show he died of a massive heart attack."

George shook his head, almost violently. "If only I'd not brought him in myself; if only I'd phoned for an ambulance – it could be he'd still be alive."

"No; his only hope was to get to hospital very quickly. Every second was crucial. You did the correct thing in bringing him in yourself. I'm only too sorry it's ended in such sadness for you – and for Heather, of course."

"Yes – Heather." He gazed blankly into space for several seconds, then looked back at the doctor, an expression akin to horror now spreading itself across his face. "Do you know, doctor, for some reason it's only just really hit me – Heather's lost her father. How am I going to tell her? They were so close, she and Arthur. It will devastate her; and with her not being too well with the baby." He shook his head in bewilderment. "How do I tell her, doctor?"

73

"You sit her down and you tell it to her gently, but directly. You cannot give news like that in an oblique way, George – that causes more problems than it solves. Anyway, Heather will take it far better than you think. I've been her doctor a long time, so I know the kind of woman your wife is. I remember when her mother died, she was remarkable then. In fact, she carried her father and brother through that time of grief. You see, she's a young woman of quite exceptional strength and character. It's partly born in her, but also it's due to the way of life she has always led. Strong minded, independent, generally courageous women are often those born to the land which falls beneath the shadow of Dartmoor. No, Heather will be all right, George. If there's anybody to be concerned about it's Derek. He took his mother's death very badly as I intimated just now, and I've a feeling he'll find it hard to come to terms with losing his father.

"Of course, he and Arthur were always close – but it's more than that. Derek is as nice and straightforward a young fellow as you could ever wish to meet – I'm sure you've formed that opinion yourself by now George. But he tends to lack drive and initiative. He's not afraid of work, mind you, but he would rather follow than lead, and because of that he has always been happy – and relieved if truth be told – to let Arthur make all the decisions at Bray Barton. But now his father is gone, and with the other male farming member of the family – yourself – having, to be blunt, only a limited knowledge of how to run a farm, he is going to have to assume leadership qualities. He is not going to find it easy. But then, I could be wrong. Time will tell. One thing for sure, he'll not shirk on the work side. A man like Derek will attempt to bury his grief beneath a mountain of work. Still, this is no time to be standing here talking; it's time you were home with your wife. And it's best if I drive you. You've already broken the law once today – though with ample justification. It would not be quite as easy to justify you driving home. Anyway, you must do nothing to put at risk the reinstatement of your licence. It cannot be long now."

"October – as long as I don't have an attack between now and then."

"Having gone this far with nothing amiss, you should be all right now," replied Dr Conway comfortingly. He led the way out of the hospital towards his immaculate, almost new Rover parked

74

virtually opposite the main door of the building. Within a few seconds they were aboard the motor and nosing out of the hospital car park onto the main road.

"I'll get a couple of chaps from my garage – Wilson's, down on Plymouth Road – to bring the Land Rover back to Bray Barton, so that'll be one thing you'll not have to worry about."

George thanked him, and not only for that kind and helpful thought. He expressed his gratitude for the kindness, understanding and advice which the doctor had given him at this time of personal crisis. Conway brushed aside his murmurings of thanks and said, quite simply, "There's no need to thank me for doing my job, George. And death, and the coming to terms with it, is part of that job – not a part I enjoy, but one which comes my way all too frequently and will continue to do so."

The powerful car rapidly devoured the miles between Tavistock Hospital and Bray Barton, so within minutes of having left the place which housed the corpse of Arthur Maunder, the car was pulling to a halt in front of the farmhouse. George alighted, and thanked the doctor once more.

"You're welcome," he replied. "I only wish I was bringing you home to perform a more pleasant task. But it has to be done, I'm afraid, and you, being the man she loves, are the one to do it. And she will take it bravely – as I said earlier. With some folk in this situation, I would ensure I was on hand in case sedatives or similar were needed – or just to provide a shoulder to weep on. But whilst that shoulder, and my medical skills, are always there if you need them, this is a time, I am certain, when the two of you will be best left to come to terms with it in your own way."

He smiled, nodded, and eased the car through the dusty yard and out onto the road leaving his passenger to brace himself to impart to the wife he loved so dearly, possibly the worst news she had ever known in her life.

Chapter Ten

Heather took the news even more stoically than George had expected. When he had told her, she merely asked him to make them both some tea, then slumped onto a hard chair at the kitchen table. Her husband did as she bid him, then, giving her a large mugful of strong, sweet tea, sat opposite her at the table. She said not a word for several minutes; rather, she just sipped from the mug and gazed vaguely into space. At last, her cup empty, she placed it onto the table and looked at her husband. "It must have been a terrible afternoon for you, George," said she in what was little more than a whisper. "Poor Dad collapsing like that and only you there to help him. It must have been dreadful, I expect you're feeling the effects of it now."

"Never mind me, Heather, my love; it's you we've to worry about. What with this dreadful, dreadful business and the baby due in less than three months – it's you we've got to care for." He stopped abruptly, realising there was no 'we' – there was just him. He would have to watch over her himself, help her through her grief, nurse her through the inevitable reaction to the death of a dearly loved father. And all of it at a time when she was becoming ever more vulnerable, both emotionally and physically, as she moved inexorably onwards towards the birth of their child. It was, though, as if she could read his thoughts.

"I will be able to come to terms with father's death, George." Her voice was steady, if rather flat in tone. "I won't grieve, darling. He wouldn't have wanted that. He lived all his life near or on the moors and that's where he died; too soon, of course, much too soon. But he came from that soil and now he will go back to it."

She reached out and took her husband's hand in hers. "I will be

76

brave, George – very brave. And I will be so for you, for our baby – and for Dad. He would not have wanted me to weep over him. He'd have wanted me to put any energies and emotions towards seeing to Bray Barton, to looking after you – he thought the world of you – and to bringing a fine healthy child into our lives. So that is what I shall do."

She got up from the table, topped up the teapot and then refilled their mugs. No sooner had she replaced them on the table than she had uttered a low shriek and put her hands to her mouth. She looked at her husband, her face even more distraught than it had been moments before. "Derek," she cried. "We must tell Derek." She shook her head, then buried it in her hands. Within seconds those hands were down by her side, and her face registered an expression of reasonable composure. "Or, to be more exact, I must tell him. It's my job, not yours."

"Perhaps we'll go up and see him together," replied George, gently. "Support for each other."

She nodded. "Yes, perhaps that'll be best. But I must tell him – it'll be better coming from me. Oh, but it'll be so hard, George. I don't know how he will take it. He and Dad were so close. And he worshipped Dad in his own phlegmatic way. But it has to be done – and done now. We must get up to see him now before he hears the news from somebody else; that would be dreadful."

Within a few minutes they were in the Jag and driving slowly towards the village, both bracing themselves against the moment when they would have to give grievous news to a quite vulnerable young man.

Derek took the tidings with more fortitude than his sister had anticipated, but she was well aware that he kept himself emotionally together by exercising enormous will. Of one thing she was certain – he was not to be left on his own that night, which would have been the case with Elaine and baby Louise still at the maternity home. So she insisted he return with George and herself – which was what he did, and was relieved to do, remaining there until his wife and first born came home to help fill their cottage.

The funeral of Arthur Maunder took place in Peter Tavy Church on a thundery July morning, the sultry air engulfing mourners like a shroud. The church was full, with relatives and hill farmers there in abundance to say a final farewell to one of their kind, a liked and respected man who had fought Bray Barton's grudging acres and the unforgiving moor all of his life and had the satisfaction of knowing neither had ever beaten him.

Derek negotiated the harrowing day with stoicism and courage, and Heather likewise until a few hours after the burial, when the last of the mourners had left Bray Barton following the traditional funeral repast. Alone in the big sitting-room with just her husband – Derek having gone out to tend to some stock – she broke down suddenly, and wept more bitterly than George could ever have imagined. The tears flowed down her pallid cheeks like raindrops coursing a window. Several minutes passed before she stopped and when she did so, she did so instantly. For a few seconds she sat in her chair gazing into space, then turned to her husband and smiled wanly.

"I'm all right now, dear," she said softly. "I've come to terms with it. I'll not cry again."

"There's nothing wrong with crying," murmured George. "After all, you've just lost your father – reason enough to cry."

"I know – and I have cried; but I'll cry no more. Dad would not have wanted me to. He was a positive man, always looking on the bright side of things, always looking for tomorrow – unusual in a farmer I suppose. So that's what we must do – and there's so much to look forward to. Our baby, of course – and our love for each other. That's tomorrow – as well as being yesterday and today. In fact, our love for each other is life itself – or it is as far as I'm concerned. And there's Bray Barton. We've got to keep it as Dad always did – and even improve it if we can. This place has been in our family for generations, George. We've never owned it, of course, and I don't suppose we ever will. But we have always treated it as if we had title to every square yard of it. Generations of Maunders have built it the way it is, year after year, decade after decade, each one adding and improving. Dad had a great feeling and understanding for that. He saw himself as a link in a long unbroken chain down the years – and would see us as the next link, with our baby being the one to follow, and so on. Don't you see, George?"

Her husband nodded.

"It'll not be easy, dear," she continued, "especially for you, not being born to this way of life; in fact not being involved in it at all until you had retired from another career. But you will cope with it, I know you will – you and Derek together. And I'll do my share, of course, after the baby's born. I'm never happier than when I am out on the land, as you know. It'll be a challenge without Dad there to guide us, but it's one we will meet; I do believe that together there is nothing we cannot overcome."

He took her in his arms and held her tightly; then releasing her, he gazed into her eyes, full of life and hope despite her grief. What could he say to this lovely young woman who brought such joy to his life? Could he tell her he was terrified of the responsibility which now fell upon his shoulders; could he tell her, at that moment, he wished he was a thousand miles away from Bray Barton and the never ending slog, and decision making, which was farming life; could he tell her that he did not feel capable of facing the challenge, as she put it, which was about to come their way with a vengeance? The answer was simplicity itself – he could not. He would have to brace himself and try to meet it all head on; for not to do so would lessen him dramatically in the eyes of this woman whose love had rescued his life from an early, long and pointless old age.

The weeks following the funeral saw George Tennant throw himself into his work as he had never before done during his entire life. This was not merely inspired by a wish to impress his wife or assuage his self-respect – though both were causes of high profile. The brutal truth was that the running of Bray Barton was a task which required more manpower than was available. For during the previous two years, the numbers of breeding ewes and store cattle had been increased by a sizeable amount – there being more to draw a living from the place when George had married Heather – but with the workforce of Arthur, his son-in-law and Derek, plus Heather making a major contribution both in the house and on the farm, the individual work load had remained roughly the same. Now, however, the most experienced farmer amongst them was no longer there, whilst Heather, because of her ever more apparent pregnancy, was able to do little on the farm. Also, Derek, though by no means shirking his work, was not the young man he had been. For as Doctor Conway had predicted, Derek had taken his father's demise very badly indeed, and without the leadership of that older man, his contribution to Bray Barton had declined by a considerable and worrying degree. He was, though, still looking to the leadership of someone older –

George – which alarmed the 'townie', a point he made to his wife.

"Derek looks to me to give a lead, Heather; to decide what should be done every day; simply to make virtually all the decisions. Yet he knows vastly more about farming than I do, even though he's so much younger. He was born to the land – has spent his entire life on it, here at Bray Barton. He has, even at his age, forgotten more than I have learnt. Yet he leaves me to run the place. He makes his contribution in terms of labour, mind you, I will say no other. But I know so little about farming, if I'm honest. I am learning, naturally; I learn every day. But there is so much to know; more than that – there is so much to understand, to feel, to simply absorb. After all, this farming business is far more than a job – it's a way of life."

Heather had agreed with him when he had made the rather passionate statement and had decided there and then to do something to help her rather beleaguered husband, who appeared suddenly to have aged with the worry of a responsibility he was not qualified to carry. So one Saturday morning in mid-September, she left Bray Barton in the Jaguar telling George she was going shopping in the village. She was, though, much longer than she would have been normally, which induced considerable worry in George, she being little more than a month away from the forecast birth of their baby. About half past midday, however, she drove the Jag into the yard, and was soon in the kitchen being confronted by a worried, and a trifle sharp tongued husband.

"Where have you been, Heather?" he demanded. "I've been worried to death."

"Why?" came the calm, assured reply.

"Surely it's obvious why. I mean, in your condition you're so – so – so vulnerable. I thought something dreadful had happened to you." Suddenly tears oozed from his eyes, rolling down his cheeks. "I worry about you so much, you know."

"Oh George, you are silly." She kissed him gently. "Come and sit down, darling – I've something to tell you."

She led him over to a small sofa on the far side of the room, and they sat down beside each other. She took both his hands in hers, and gazed into his careworn face. "You look so tired – and worried, as well. It's the farm, of course. You've really been pitched in at the deep end, Dad no longer being with us."

He shrugged his shoulders. "Well, I reckon I'll get a grip on it all one day," he replied. "Though I hope that's sooner rather than later."

"I'm sure you are right. The trouble is, though, that you will wear yourself out doing it. What you need is a very experienced man beside you who can both work hard and advise with the benefit of that experience; and I've the very man in mind if you are agreeable – and Derek, obviously. Frank Morton is his name. You probably know him by sight – a thick-set fellow, almost bald, about forty-five years old. His wife helps out behind the bar at the pub now and again. Well, Frank worked for poor old farmer Dingle up at Moorgate – about a mile up the road from here. Cold barren place it is as you may well know. Frank went there as a boy just left school and worked there for the greater part of thirty years. He would be there still but farmer Dingle died of a severe stroke about three years ago, and within six months Mrs Dingle had sold the place, lock, stock and barrel – glad to be out of it, she said. Well, unfortunately for Frank, the fellow who bought it – Henry Gibson; he's there now – has two sons home with him on the farm so he didn't need to hire any labour. Thus Frank had to go, and he didn't like it. Nor would any man who had spent most of his life on the land as had Frank. Sadly he wasn't able to get a job on a farm locally – not many men are employed on the land these days as you well know – so he went to Tavistock to work in a factory. The job's easier and the money's better, according to Frank, and I wouldn't doubt it. Yet, I've heard him say many times in the pub that he would dearly like to be back on the land. So I went to the village this morning to see him and luckily found him at home – in his garden – and I asked him if he would consider working at Bray Barton. You would think I'd told him he had won the pools. It's a long time since I saw a man look as happy. Anyway, the long and the short of it is he would love to work here. So I told him I would come home, see what you and Derek think about it, and would let him know before the day was out. If we offer him the job, he'll put his notice in regarding the factory job on Monday morning. So what do you think, George? He's an absolutely first class man. In fact, he probably knows almost as much about hill farming as Dad did. If he had only had some capital to set himself up, I don't doubt he would have made a first class farmer. I believe if we take him on, it will be one of the wisest moves we ever make. And we can afford him, dear, if you're worried about that. Poor old Dad's not drawing anything out of the place these days, is he?"

"Yes, you're right," agreed her husband. "You're right about everything, Heather – as always. We can afford him, and we certainly need him. So if he's willing to come, then take him on. A man with his experience and knowledge will be a Godsend. In fact, it will make me feel ten years younger. The responsibility of running this place during the two months since your Dad died has been enormous – or at least, it has been so far as I'm concerned. I've been used to responsibility, naturally, running my own business for years. But that was in a field I knew inside out. This farming game is still quite a mystery to me, yet every day I am expected to make decisions which affect the running of the place – and our livelihood. It's like making bricks without straw. Your Frank Morton cannot start soon enough for me. And I reckon when you speak to Derek, he'll fully back up what I have said."

Derek, his diffident nature making it virtually impossible for him to make major decisions at Bray Barton, did indeed agree with what George had said, and was truly delighted to welcome to the farm the help and experience of a tough, wily countryman used to the uncertain, hard working ways of hill farming.

Chapter Eleven

Thus it was that on a fresh, sunny September morning, a feeling of autumn already in the air, that Frank Morton started working at Bray Barton; and his coming was salvation to them right from the first day. For it was obvious he had forgotten more than George had ever learnt – probably twice over – and possessed a decisiveness which Derek would never acquire. Not that he actually made decisions – that was not his place. Rather, he pointed his employers in the direction of actions and decisions which, invariably, were correct.

Heather, of course, possessed a similar ability, plus a comprehensive knowledge of the day to day running of Bray Barton, but by virtue of age had not the experience of Morton and by virtue of her condition, and busy life within the house, had not the opportunity to exhibit her knowledge.

George Tennant was now feeling better than he had for a very long time. Frank's subtle guidance in the everyday running of things had taken an enormous weight from off his shoulders, whilst Heather's ever increasing pregnancy was now becoming ever more important to him. For, at last, he was really looking forward to becoming a father again, despite the generation gap since previously he had been in such a position.

So on a nippy morning in early October, just a week prior to Heather's 'due day' he strode from the farmyard, out across a couple of wide fields to see that all was well with a dozen or so fine bullocks destined for Tavistock Goose Fair the following week, a spring in his step and nothing but confidence for the future within him. He eventually reached the far field and cast his ever more perceptive eyes over the splendid light brown beasts which cropped the grass. He smiled; as good a bunch of bullocks as existed in Devon, he mused, and they would surely fetch a good price at the Fair the following Wednesday. He was about to surmise just how much they would make, when all thought of cattle suddenly left his brain; in fact, all thought and consciousness departed his mind as he flopped forward into the thick grass.

How long he was there he knew not, but thought it was little more than seconds as the nearby bullocks, rasping the succulent grass, seemed not to have moved at all. The time, though, was irrelevant; for the one ghastly thought which hammered at his brain was that after almost two years, after serving all but ten days of his 'sentence' of no driving licence, he had had another attack – so would have to start again, a further brace of years without being able to drive on the roads. He buried his head in his hands; nobody knew just how much he had yearned to have his licence restored to him. He had felt a prisoner – and somewhat inadequate – without it, and now, after happily looking forward to its restoration before the end of the month, he was surely destined to remain a prisoner.

He lifted his head from his hands, the despair evaporating suddenly. For this was a lonely spot; nobody had seen him collapse save for the hungry stock, and they were far more interested in the grass than they were in him. And who was to say that it was the epilepsy which had made him pass out. After all, he took his tablets every day, and such medication had kept him free from attacks for a very long time. Perhaps it was something else which had made him collapse. He had had a couple of late nights tending a sick steer, and some early mornings. It could simply be he was over-tired. Yes, that was it; could happen to anybody. He would have a few early nights – then he would be fine. And as for the faint, he wouldn't bother anybody with that. It was, after all, just one of those silly things – and would not happen again.

He got to his feet, shook his still muzzy head as would a dog coming in from the rain, and made for home, his decision of a few minutes earlier laying easier upon his conscience than it should have done.

Indeed, that conscience was totally dormant when he received back his licence just a fortnight afterwards.

Nicola Heather Tennant came into the world on November seventh, three weeks later than expected, and even then she did not arrive naturally. For her mother's increasingly problematical pregnancy climaxed in the baby being delivered by Caesarian section, the need for such surgery leading the gynaecologist to advise George that his wife should have the minor operation which would prevent her from having further children.

The decision for him was simplicity itself. For whilst he felt infinitely greater joy at the safe birth of his lovely daughter than he had ever thought possible – his worries over his age and the responsibility which was to be thrust back onto his shoulders at a time when he previously had considered all such things long past having abated somewhat – there was no doubt in his mind that the welfare of his dear wife was paramount. So he readily agreed with the doctor when it was pointed out the dangers to Heather's health – indeed, her life – if she were to attempt to have another child, and promised he would endeavour to convince his wife.

That, though, proved impossible. For Heather was adamant she was going to have at least one more baby. "I do not believe in only children, George," she opined simply, lying wan and weak in her hospital bed a couple of days after the birth. "It's just not fair on them. What I do believe is that a farmer should have at least one son. So I'm willing to agree that if our next baby is a boy, then I will have this operation." That was her decision and George knew her well enough to realise it was final.

The months which followed the birth were good ones for the Tennants as a family. Nicola, naturally, was doted upon, especially by a father who felt – and wanted to be – more involved in the rearing of his offspring than he had when Martin and Alison had been of similar age, long years ago, whilst Heather, although slow to recover from the traumas of the birth, was looking more her old self by Christmas. Her spirit and zest for life had in no way been diminished at all. And George had regained his driving licence – and realised when it was returned to him, the full extent to which he had missed it. For quite apart from its importance to him as a farmer living in a lonely rural area, it made him feel much better concerning himself. He had spent years dependent on others, cadging lifts and so on – at times even walking quite long distances – when it came to travel. Now, though, the car or Land Rover keys were in his pocket and the ability to exercise greater control over his life was within his grasp once more. And along with this came confidence. For here

85

he was, a man well into his fifties – just a few years earlier retired, widowed and facing, probably, a long, barren time of it before the Grim Reaper made his inevitable call – now married to a lovely young woman. Also he was the father of a gorgeous baby daughter, who grew to look more like her mother daily – whilst her seemingly constant smiling and laughter gave irrefutable evidence she had also inherited Heather's personality – and he was the joint tenant of a fine Devonshire farm here in the foothills of Dartmoor. Fate, though notoriously fickle, would appear to be treating him in a benevolent fashion at present.

Having said this, however, he could be forgiven for feeling that fate was not being totally kind. For early in December an atrocious spell of wet and windy weather stormed across the West Country, the rain falling with a consistent intensity George had never before known during his entire life. Derek said that he had experienced likewise wet spells, but he doubted they had continued for quite as long a period. Certainly day in, day out, the rains, carried on shrieking south-westerly gales homing in from the Atlantic, doused the West Country, causing flooding problems said by many older folk to be the worst they had known. Bray Barton, sited on the long, mainly gradual slope which stretched down from the moors above to the River Tavy below, was never in danger of actually being flooded, but its fields were riven by cascading streams of water which poured off the rocky, thin soiled moors and thundered their way with startling speed in virtually straight lines through large tracts of the farm – a couple traversing the farm yard itself, though none, mercifully, flowing near the house – and on through the holding which lay below and then into the raging, peat black Tavy. The river thundered onwards to hurtle through Tavistock, and cascade its mighty load into the Tamar near Bere Ferrers. Thence, at a more leisurely pace, it would swirl to the sea beyond Plymouth.

This deluge continued into the New Year, through January and into February. It meant that the stock, and the breeding ewes brought down from the moors prior to lambing in March and April, had to be watched constantly, and fed. Near mid-February, though, the winds turned from south-westerlies to north-easterlies – and the rains turned to snow. Fortunately the falls were not heavy but that which did lay was sustained by the bitter winds and frosts; thus the fields with so much water in them plus the snow, became rock solid – nightmarish skating rinks. Feeding all the livestock and sheep occupied a very large slice of the day, whilst getting fodder up to the sheep still on the moor became a fraught business. Once again, though, Frank Morton showed his worth. Having dealt with winters of similar vein – indeed, regarding snow and frost, infinitely worse – he was encouraged by his employers to take command of the situation, and did so, as he often had before, with an ease which suggested that very few problems on the land would ever faze him.

As it was he gently but firmly guided George and the ever more retiring Derek through each day and did so in a way which ensured that the feeding of the farm animals was accomplished infinitely faster than it would have been had it been left to them – which included the carrying across the frozen landscape of the moors, by way of masterly and nerveless driving of tractor and trailer, adequate fodder for the sheep. However, there was general relief at Bray Barton – and far beyond – when the thaw came in mid-March, just before the first lambs were due. As Frank said, "We can get back to normal now. We'll have no more bad weather; it's set fair for a month – mark my words."

They did mark his words – and they were to prove highly accurate. For late March and most of April saw an unseasonably warm and dry spell of weather, ideal for the delivery of an above average crop of lambs that were soon eagerly filling their bellies on the fast growing grass.

So, as he went in for lunch on a lovely day towards the end of April, George Tennant felt happy with life. In less than an hour, however, the world of Heather and himself, which had seemed settled at last, was once again in turmoil.

He closed the kitchen door behind him and was surprised to see Derek sitting at the table. His brother-in-law invariably went home to have lunch with Elaine and little Louise, his pride and joy, unless there was a crisis at the farm. Instantly, a feeling of foreboding overcame him. He had always been something of a pessimist and thus quick to espy signs of ill omen. The fact that Derek's breaking of routine might have meant unexpected good news never crossed his mind. He washed his hands at the kitchen sink, then sat down in his customary place at the big table, facing his wife, Derek to his right. Heather deftly piled high two plates with shepherd's pie – she always ate as much as her husband with no adverse affect to her figure – placed them on the table, then sat down in her chair. George, seeing that Derek had but a cup of tea before him, looked questioningly across at him. "Not having something to eat, Derek?"

"No thanks, George," replied his brother-in-law. "Don't feel very hungry, to be honest. I had a good breakfast and, I suppose, haven't done enough this morning to work it off."

"Well, you're welcome – you know that."

"Oh, yes – I know George."

Heather swallowed her mouthful. "Derek says there's something he wants to say to us, dear."

"Well, get it off your chest, then, Derek." George said the words in as relaxed a fashion as he was able, but there was, within him, growing at an alarming pace, conviction that nothing but bad news was going to flow from Derek Maunder's lips.

"I think it best if I wait until you've both finished your meal. It's just something I want to chat to you both about so it's not exactly fair of me to expect you to ruin your dinner just to talk about my problems, when ten minutes is not going to make a huge amount of difference. I'll just top up my tea cup, and then perhaps we can have a chat when you've both finished."

If ever a statement was guaranteed to cause indigestion, it was this from Derek. For the couple, their hearts in their mouths, along with the shepherd's pie, just gobbled down their meals, excellent food turned to sawdust in their mouths by this enigmatic, but depressing, promise of news to come from their guest. George was to say afterwards that it seemed the longest time he had ever spent eating a meal in his life, though, in reality, it was probably amongst the shortest. Whatever, he and Heather cleared their plates at virtually the same moment, spurned the large fruit cake which sat in highly appetising splendour on the table, topped up their cups and turned again, almost simultaneously, to look at Derek, whose embarrassment at the entire situation had grown by the second.

"Right – we're all ears," said his sister, with a brightness in her voice which did not accurately reflect her feelings. She knew her brother better than anyone. His coming to see them in this way was the culmination of weeks of thought and, probably, worry. Never a man to confide easily, if at all, there had to be some major cause for his visit this day, and it would be bad news for them he would impart. Derek drained his cup, and placed it back onto the saucer. Then, his eyes gazing unblinkingly down onto the table top, he explained himself.

"Well, as you know, Elaine's dad's brother, Uncle Billy, emigrated to Canada many years ago; not long after the war, in fact, when he was little more than a lad. Did well too, for after working on a few farms during his early years there, he got enough money together, somehow, to buy his own. As he was a good farmer, and a shrewd man, he was able over the years, to add regularly to his land and stock and suchlike; so when he died a couple of years ago, he left a large prospering farm to Danny, his only son – his only child, in fact. 'Course you will have met Danny; he was over here for our wedding – what, three years ago now I suppose. Whilst he was here we had a good chat and he said that if ever in the future I felt like a change of farming from our way to the Canadian way – and there is a colossal difference, inevitably, with the amount of land they have got to play with – then I should contact him, for he would love us to come over for, well," he shrugged his shoulders, "perhaps a year or two, or possibly even permanently . . ."

"And you have decided to go," interjected Heather, in even tones, the words in the form of a statement rather than a question.

Her brother nodded, and looked at her directly for the first time. There was still a touch of guilt and embarrassment about him but this had been partly superseded with a mild confidence – rare in Derek. "You see, it's not been the same for me here without Dad. Not that I'm criticising you in any way, Heather," he added, hastily. "No man could ever have, or have had, a better sister than you. And I've never met a nicer man than you, George – I mean that. No, it's me who's to blame. You see, all of my life Dad was there – in my school-days and, in recent times, in my working life. We always got on so well, as you know. He was always there for advice, for help – for leadership as well I suppose. And, of course, he was a master of his craft – and that I found so very important. Sadly, I am not – nor ever will be, if I'm honest. I should improve as I get older, mind you, but the thought that one day I might have to take on the full responsibility of running Bray Barton – after all, if nothing unforeseen happens, George, you will retire long before I do – well, it frightens the life out of me to be frank."

"But Dad would have retired as well, Derek," his sister interjected.

"Yes, I know. But in the normal course of things he could have been expected to have lived well into his seventies at least, so he would have been there to advise me – or, at least, until I was well into middle age. But now he's gone I've nobody to turn to – and I mean no disrespect to you George, I'm sure you realise that."

"I do, Derek. It's no more than the truth, after all. I didn't know a fleece of wool from a cow's horn until I had turned fifty; so my knowledge of farming – especially the tough ways of it around these parts – are scant to say the least."

"Yes, yes that's right," agreed his brother-in-law, eagerly, George's understanding words being balm to a conscience which was troubling him greatly. For he was only too well aware that he was not only intending to turn his back on commitments he had, morally, to his much loved sister and her hard working if inexperienced husband, he was also turning away from his birthplace and birth right – a Maunder, and named so, had worked Bray Barton's exacting, but precious acres as tenant master for well over a century. Derek took a deep breath like a high diver about to make the plunge, and proceeded to rather gabble out a statement he had been preparing in his head for some time.

"It all came to a head about three weeks ago, when Danny phoned to see how Elaine's and his mutual uncle was – Uncle Percy – who, as you know, had a bad heart attack about a month back; but I really believe he phoned to ask me about the suggestion he made to us at the time of our wedding. Apparently he is finding it a bit difficult without his father as well, having worked with him for so many years. And on top of that, he is finding it hard to get – and keep – good staff. It seems some factory or other has been built about twenty miles from the farm, and men working on the land are leaving in their droves to go to work there because of the big money they are paying; you know, the old story. So he's asked Elaine, Louise and myself to go over there to live – for the time being, at least. They've a huge house with only his wife and himself in it – they've no children as yet – and he says we could live there entirely separate with no problem. At first I would be employed by him, of course, but if after, say a year or so, we decided we wanted to stay permanently, then he would offer us a share in the farm, though naturally he would retain the major interest. As soon as he made the offer I had the feeling that I wanted to accept it but, obviously, I needed time to think about it all and talk it through with Elaine. I thought she might be reluctant, but she's all in favour – of giving it a try at least. She feels that if things go well for us out there, the future in Canada could be better than it is here – and I fancy she could be right. I mean there are two families living off Bray Barton now, and although it's a sizeable farm by local standards, and we've the moorland rights, of course, the way the farming future is looking here with over production, the blasted Common Agricultural Policy, set aside and BSE, of course, it could be we'll be scratching around to make a living in the years to come. So, if we went, it would make things easier for you economically."

"But we would not have your labour and expertise, Derek," said his brother-in-law in as emotionless a tone of voice as he could muster, faced with what he saw as a catastrophic development. "You were born here and you've lived and worked here all your life, virtually. You know the problems, the challenge, the routines of hill farming – most of which are very different from those of farmers just a few miles down the valley where they rarely feel the north wind, and even more rarely suffer greatly from its consequences. How do we replace that, Heather and I? Granted, what little 'cake' we make at Bray Barton will end up almost entirely on our plate once you've gone to Canada, but without your expertise and knowledge, and with the farm left largely to the efforts of a 'rookie' like me, perhaps that cake will be so small we'll starve to death."

"I doubt it George," replied Derek, a gentle smile playing around his lips. "You're not as much of a greenhorn as you suggest. In fact, for a man who had scarcely seen a farm animal until a very few years ago, you amaze me the way you've picked things up. Granted, you'll probably never be an expert, but you're fortunate in the fact you're married to one. Heather knows vastly more than me, whilst Frank Morton knows more than the three of us put together. You'll be all right in that direction, although you'll possibly need to take on another man. But then, who knows, we may not like it there and come home again within twelve months."

"Does that mean you'll keep your cottage," enquired his sister, although mentally dismissing the possibility that Derek and his family would ever return to live in Devon. The greater mechanisation of a large Canadian farm, and his future role where he would have, to him, the bonus of being a junior partner without having to make any major decisions, would surely ensure that.

"For the time being," he replied. "We'll see how it goes out there first. I mean, it's no good selling your house then finding you want to come back to it. We reckon we'll rent it out for a while and when – or if – we decide we'll not be coming back, then we will put it on the market. We've enough – just – to tide us over for a little while, thanks to what Dad left me."

There was a sudden silence, lingering but seconds, seeming though like minutes in the taut atmosphere. Heather broke it.

"So that's it then, Derek."

Her brother nodded. "I suppose it is," he agreed.

"When do you go?"

"Probably early September. That'll mean the shearing and harvest will be over so I'll be able to leave with a clear conscience." The short, forced laugh, however, gave evidence that the opposite was the case. "It'll mean that we will be able to get settled in before the winter comes."

Heather nodded her understanding, whilst George merely stared blankly ahead, as he had for some minutes. Silence descended once more. This time it was broken by Derek getting noisily to his feet. "Right, I'd better be off – several things I want to do around the yard. I'm sorry to have . . ." He tailed off, realising that this news had lain waste the emotions and hopes of his sister and brother-in-law in the short term, at least, and that further mention of it now would help nobody. "See you later – thanks for the tea, Heather." He made his escape, rapidly, from the kitchen, leaving behind a somewhat bemused couple.

For a minute or more, they remained silent, Heather drinking her tea, whilst her husband continued to stare straight and unblinkingly ahead, almost trance-like. At last the farmer's wife got up from the table and began to clear away the dishes to the sink. That done, she picked up the teapot and poured the remainder into the two cups – sole occupants of the table top now – and then sat down opposite her husband.

"I suppose I should have seen it coming," she said.

"What do you mean?" The voice sounded flat – almost

defeated.

"Derek. I knew that he would never really come to terms with Dad's passing, but assumed that time would put it right to some degree. It seems I was wrong. He is going because he feels he will never be able to truly cope here – and I doubt he'll be back."

"You're right there – which leaves us in a mess which scarcely bears thinking about."

"Well, it gives us a few problems, yes – but nothing we cannot overcome."

"What the hell do you mean, Heather? A few problems? Derek's the senior partner in terms of experience; he also knows ten times as much about farming as the other male partner; me; and something else, which he didn't mention – was afraid to at present, I don't wonder – but will one day, is how much he will require when he formally gives up his partnership in the farm. Because that's what will happen. When he gets settled in Canada – as he will, we both know that – he'll want a fair amount of money to make some sort of investment into Danny's place which he will surely wish and be expected to do. And when he comes to us to buy out his share in Bray Barton, what do we do for money? I know we've still got a fair sum remaining after the sale of my house, but with making up that shortfall of sixty thousand pounds on Martin's guarantee and drawing on it for various things, that amount has been seriously diminished. And what remains needs to be set aside for us for the future – along with those few thousands your dad left you. My old age is not that far away, being brutally realistic, and we've got a young daughter's future to think about. And the only money we will ever make is what we can glean from farming Bray Barton; we obviously can never sell it or any part of it even if we wanted to, seeing as the Duchy own every square yard of the place; which I accept we would probably never wish to do anyway," he added hastily, realising such talk of getting rid of her birthplace could well upset his wife. "But the question remains, Heather – when Derek comes to us to buy him out, where will we get the money from?"

"Nowhere, George – that's the answer to the question. It will be he who breaks the partnership, not us. So he'll be bought out if and when we wish to do so. It will certainly make sense to buy him out one day, if only to ensure the farm remains in the family – our family, that is; little Nicola and her brother when he comes along. For heaven's sake, George, don't always be so pessimistic – think things through." Anger was exceedingly rarely a soul-mate of Heather's, especially where her husband was concerned, but there were times when the negative attitudes which – she became increasingly aware – were very much part of his nature, both exasperated and antagonised her.

"I have thought things through, Heather – what do you think I've been doing here for the past few minutes," he retorted testily. "The fact is that even with Derek, Frank and myself, we seem to be on the go all hours sent. With Derek gone, there's no way we can cope. And, possibly even worse, he – though not the same as your dad, of course – has far more knowledge of, and feeling for, farming than he will ever admit to himself, whereas I am still very much an apprentice. I just do not know how I am going to run the place on my own, I truly don't."

"But you're not going to run the place on your own, George. I'm here to help – and I can still do my share outside despite having Nicola and the house to look after – and, of course, there's Frank. As Derek so rightly said, he knows more than the three of us put together."

"But we'll still be a pair of hands short."

"Then we take on another man. Granted, good farm workers are not thick on the ground, especially when they've got to work close to, and on, the moors. But they are about – so we will find one."

George Tennant shook his head. "It's not that simple is it. I . . ."

Heather jumped to her feet, knocking her chair over in the process and crashed her right hand down onto the table – so hard the noise would have been heard out in the yard, and would have caused her very real pain had not it been anaesthetised by anger.

"It is that simple. We just take on another man and carry on as before. And although you'll be the boss out there on the farm, you listen to Frank Morton. That does not mean to say you do everything he suggests, but you would need very good reason for not doing so. You delegate, George. Good God, when you were a successful businessman years ago, you must have delegated."

"Yes, of course I did. But then I knew what I was delegating. And I also knew that, with the odd exception, the jobs I did push onto somebody else were things I could do myself – and do well. With this bloody farming business, I'm only too well aware that just about every man, woman and possibly even child around here, no matter whether they're on the land or not, probably knows how to farm better than I do." He was angry himself, now, though he managed to keep himself from shouting at the wife whom he loved but who, at such times as these, really did not seem to appreciate just how difficult things were for him.

As if reading his thoughts, Heather retorted, "I know it's not easy for you, George – and I do sympathise to a degree. But that's no good, is it – 'sympathy without relief is like mustard without beef', as my mother used to say. You've taken this farm on – you've taken me on. We have a lovely daughter, and I do hope before very much longer we'll have a lovely son as well. We've so much to be grateful for and happy about. But life is a roller coaster – up and down, up and down all the way through; and it will come up again – invariably it does. The thing to do is to fight when it goes against you. George, you don't seem to fight. Things go along quite nicely for a while and you're happy with life, but come a bad spell and you want to give in. I'm ashamed of you, I saw you as a man of character, of substance – even of courage. I'm beginning to think my judgement was sadly wrong, and that your love for Nicola and myself is shallow."

No sooner had the words left her lips than she regretted them. Not that he did not deserve them; it was just that there were times he appeared to be as vulnerable as a child and needed comforting more than scolding. Yet, that stinging rebuke proved to be amongst the best words she was ever to speak to him.

For almost instantly, amidst the sullen, somewhat self-pitying expression which dominated his face, a look of alarm appeared. "You don't really mean that, Heather?" His voice was pregnant with emotion – and perhaps a touch of fear.

His wife looked at him for several seconds, then gazed away, her very real anger with him temporarily making a prisoner of her tongue. He, though, became more animated and agitated than she had ever before seen him – possibly more so than anybody had witnessed during a large part of his lifetime.

Suddenly he jumped up from the table, hurtled around to the opposite side and took his wife by the shoulders. "Heather, please say you don't mean that," he implored, "please. I love you – and Nicola – so much. You two are everything which makes life for me worthwhile. Please do not doubt that – now, or ever."

Heather gazed at him briefly, her face registering little emotion. Then she slid her arms around his neck and pulled him to her; she kissed him then looked up at his worried, almost stricken face. "I don't doubt it, George. I know that we are loved as much as any two people have ever been loved. And I am sorry for what I said. It was one of those things easily uttered in the heat of the moment and regretted for a long time afterwards. It's just that I want you to have more confidence in yourself – to realise you are more of a success at your new way of life than you believe. I do so want you to understand just how much you have in you to give – to me, to Nicola, to the way we live. You're a good man – and a wise one as well. Believe in yourself and you can make Bray Barton even better than Dad made it. That will not be easy, mind you, but you most certainly can do it, with your business experience and, to a major degree, your greater knowledge and understanding of the wider world, having spent the bulk of your life outside farming."

He shook his head. "No, Heather, I don't think so. Much as I would like to, I feel it's all beyond me."

"You never know what is or is not beyond you till you try, do you?"

"No – that's true enough."

"Then try, George, that is all I ask of you – try, fight, do not give in. Will you do that for me?"

He looked into her beautiful, but tear-stained face and nodded – first gently then earnestly. Choking back the deep emotion he felt within himself, he uttered the words she longed to hear, "Yes, I will try and I will fight; and I will make a farmer – some day."

Chapter Twelve

George and Heather were fortunate in recruiting a first class fellow to work on Bray Barton within less than two months of Derek stating his intention to leave. Indeed, so quickly did they find him, and so anxious were they to employ him, that they took the man on at least a month before they would ideally have wished with Derek still involved in the day to day running of the farm; the young man came onto the job market at that time, however, and they knew that if they did not snap him up immediately then somebody else would, most assuredly.

Phil Miller was a burly young fellow of some twenty-five years who as a farmer's son, had been born and bred to the land. His father, Jack, farmed Holly Park, which lay adjacent the moor a mile or so from Bray Barton. It was a hard working, windswept wedge of land with the farmhouse and buildings lying some four hundred feet higher than those of Bray Barton – which made it a raw place indeed in the winter. Yet Heather, and her father Arthur before her, had always fancied Holly Park. One of the attractions of the place was that it was not owned by the Duchy as was Bray Barton and so many other farms in the parish; no, Jack Miller owned Holly Park and was ever proud of the fact. Arthur Maunder – and his daughter – had always longed to farm that which they owned but were realistic enough to know that money in the amounts necessary to buy even a modest place like Holly Park would probably never come their way.

But the freehold was not the only attraction regarding the holding; Heather had said often to George that she felt the farm had a potential which, hard working though he was, Jack Miller had never exploited. He had always been inclined to do things on the cheap, whereas Heather, had it been her farm, would have fed the land more generously in terms of fertiliser, would have given the buildings much needed attention, would have improved the quality of the stock – and would, ultimately, have gained reward in terms of both satisfaction and increased profit. Even as it was, though, Holly Park was a reasonably neat farm, tolerably level for a Devon holding backing onto Dartmoor, and had views over the moors which were little short of breathtaking. Thus, Heather Tennant's desire to own it, though she was aware it would almost certainly never be satisfied, remained alive within her, nonetheless.

It was, of course, a farm of sufficient size to accommodate the labour and skills of the farmer's son, and for several years it had done so, with Phil working for his father on leaving school. However, there were problems in this, for although both were able men, each had a temper which could explode at the speed of light, and during the years they had spent an all too great, and increasing, proportion of their working lives at each other's throats. And as Phil got older, his temper grew along with his confidence, and confrontations between himself and his father – most of them the fault of the progressively aggressive younger man – became ever more common, a situation which caused increasing grief to Jack's wife, and Phil's mother, Sally Miller.

Basically an easy going woman, Sally had, nevertheless, a core of steel within her, and when the chips were down she could be more than a match for her tempestuous husband and son. Thus it was, after one particularly explosive row between father and son which saw them framing up to each other, Sally laid down the law – with a contained, but deep anger which brooked no opposition. And her law was simple enough – Phil could continue to live at Holly Park if he wished – but he would not be allowed to work there any longer on a full-time basis. Being their only son – indeed, their only child – he would inherit Holly Park when they died, of course; in fact, it could be they would hand it over to him, lock stock and barrel when they retired, if they could afford to; for despite his faults in terms of temper and moods, he was an efficient young man who would possibly make a good farmer. But until that day came he would have to work for somebody else, though he was welcome – indeed expected, if he remained at home, to do odds and ends on the farm during evenings and weekends to earn his keep.

Thus it was that the tempestuous – at times almost dangerous – Phil Miller came onto the job market. He quickly obtained a job working for Henry Billings who farmed Blackmoor, a sizeable place little more than a stone's throw from Holly Park. Everything went smoothly for some time, with the ageing Billings pleased to have a strong, willing, tolerably responsible and knowledgeable young man about the farm who could turn his hand to virtually everything. As for Phil, he settled in quite well with a boss who allowed him to use much of his own initiative – of which he had a goodly amount – about his work. The problem was that Farmer Billings, though basically a very genuine sort of man, had a fault well known in the parish – he was exceedingly mean; and he made the grave error of allowing his natural trait to overcome his better judgement, by attempting to cheat Phil Miller. On a couple of occasions the worker had had to point out to his employer that his pay packet was short due to the fact he had worked more overtime than the farmer had credited him. Billings had claimed 'errors' and had paid him the amount short, but Phil, knowing his employer's reputation, decided to keep the closest of eyes on what was due to him.

Thus when it happened that less than a month after the farmer's previous efforts to short change him, he tried it again – and to the tune of over thirty pounds – the volatile young man's temper snapped, and hurling abuse at Billings, he walked out on him never to return. Consequently he again came onto the job market and advised of this fact by Frank Morton within twenty-four hours of it happening, George and Heather immediately offered him employment at Bray Barton. The young man was more than happy to accept.

"We've done a good job today, George," Heather had opined immediately following their 'capture' of Phil Miller. "Of course, he'll go back and work with his father one day – or I would think so, anyway. After all, no man's going to be an employee for ever when he can be his own boss. But I fancy it could be a few years yet before he is ready to do so. And with his temperament, and the wildness there has undoubtedly always been within him, and probably always will be – the leopard doesn't change his spots, as the saying goes – there's no guarantee he will ever be able to farm successfully on his own. That though, is his business; and it's all probably some way to the future."

Thus Phil Miller came to work at Bray Barton during the last week of June, and immediately showed his worth by his ability to handle heavy bales of hay with a speed and ease which even Frank Morton had never before seen. As for Morton himself, George, listening as he usually did to Heather, gave him the title of Farm Manager and raised his pay by twenty per cent.

"I'm not really sure we can afford it," she had said, "but he is certainly worth it – more, if truth be told – and the title of Manager is no meaningless one, because he does manage the place. After all, we rarely do anything here before taking his advice – and it's seldom wrong."

For his part, Frank Morton was delighted with the pay rise and virtually speechless when it came to his new title. He had never seen himself being anything other than an honest, hard working man who would always have to earn his crust with the use of his hands. And nothing would change. But self-esteem is ever important and there was no doubt the title of Farm Manager was a major boost to his confidence.

Heather shed tears when her brother, sister-in-law and niece came to bid their farewells on a rainy day in September. For she was certain within herself that whilst she would most probably see them again sometime in the future, it could be many years hence – and then only fleetingly. For she felt that once they had become settled in Canada, they would find the easier, more affluent way of life too good to leave – and she knew sufficient of the world to be only too well aware that farming on a massive scale in the New World, though not without problems, meant less physical work, and infinitely greater rewards than the working of a rocky holding in the foothills of Dartmoor. And she had a feeling that Derek was also aware of this, for he was at pains to add to his promise that 'we'll be back', the words 'if only for a visit.' So he, Elaine and Louise bade their farewells and headed for their new life more than three thousand miles away, leaving behind a sister and brother-in-law who, whilst sad at their departure, had now come to terms with it both in the personal and the working sense.

Less than a fortnight after Derek and family had left for Canada, the Tennants had unexpected visitors – indeed, highly unexpected. They had just finished eating one of the farmer's wife's customary huge and succulent Sunday dinners when there came a loud knock at the back door. George rose, heavily, from his seat at the table, muttered to his wife that he had over-eaten yet again – his weekly comment – then shuffled wearily in his slippers across the kitchen floor to the door. He opened it slowly – then forgot suddenly the fine meal which he had just devoured. For standing before him were his daughter Alison and her husband Simon.

Four years and more had passed since last he had seen them – on that fraught afternoon in Brighton when he had informed them of his intention to remarry – and the confrontation with them now was a shock, with the extreme surprise temporarily suppressing emotion. For seconds – an embarrassing, almost unforgivable period of time – he stood, his mouth slightly open, like the big kitchen door, the handle of which he clung to with his right hand, gazing at these faces from the past. How much longer his immobility of mind and body would have ruled became conjecture, for Heather, puzzled at her husband's behaviour, came across the kitchen to the door, saw her niece and nephew-in-law, recognised them instantly even though she had met them only once, and promptly invited them in, a welcoming smile playing about her lips. She, though, like George, was both greatly surprised and bemused over their visit.

George, taking a grip of himself, apologised for his behaviour at the door – "It took me a few seconds to realise it was really you," he stuttered, lamely – and took the visitors into the parlour, whilst Heather prepared a tray laden with the type of fare a Devonshire farm traditionally has in abundance, scones, cream, home-made jam, a massive fruit cake, and so forth, along with a gigantic teapot and associated crockery. The guests, sitting reasonably relaxed in the large, comfortable room and hungry as they had eaten nothing since an early and spartan continental breakfast in a small hotel at the toe end of Cornwall, made laudable inroads into the very early afternoon tea laid before them, whilst their hosts, full from their Sunday lunch, merely partook of the fruits of the teapot.

The conversation was a little stilted at first, but soon began to flow with a pleasant, gentle ease, with all four making contributions as they précised the myriad happenings of the past few years since they had last met, their only communications being via the routine and dutiful ones of Christmas and birthday cards, on occasions with brief letters enclosed. In this conversation, Heather and George gave more of themselves than did their guests, the former telling of very real happenings at Bray Barton and in their lives generally, whilst Alison and Simon spoke more of trivial matters, telling the farming couple, amongst other things, that they had dropped in on them after having spent a few days touring Cornwall — "We both felt we needed something of a break," remarked Simon, with some severity. And he certainly looked as if he did, mused his father-in-law. Always a touch gaunt, the fellow now looked mildly haggard, stress, even fear appearing to haunt his face, and bringing a nervous restlessness to a man whom George remembered as always appearing calm and in control of things.

Alison though, appeared very different; in fact her father had rarely seen her look better. For about her there was contentment and happiness, and a softening of a face which had always looked a touch teasy. Indeed always basically a pretty girl when she made the effort, she now hovered on the verge of being beautiful, and there was a vibrancy about her made more apparent by the counterweight of her husband's seeming depression. Although the conversation was pleasant enough, George had a feeling there were subjects which his guests wished to broach but did not quite know how to; issues of very considerable importance to their own lives and which somehow could well affect those of the new Dartmoor farmer and his wife. He had, though, not the slightest idea of how he could steer the conversation around to such matters, especially as he had not the slightest notion of what they were.

Heather Tennant, however, had not the slightest doubt as to what the main issue of the day was, and what had brought this most unexpected visit. And in her customary bright and direct way, she cut across the prevarication and small talk and got directly to the point.

"Alison, it's very forward of me, I know," she interjected briskly, though not discourteously, "but I do believe you've got some news for us; important news — in fact, wonderful news. Am I right?"

For a few seconds Alison was rendered speechless by a directness — and perception — of which she was not accustomed, but soon took a grip of herself, smiled, nodded and said simply,

"I'm pregnant."

Heather squealed with delight, "That's lovely, Alison, it really is. I'm so happy for you – and so is George, aren't you dear?"

His wife's blunt encouragement to him to give congratulations quickly to his daughter were not needed, however, for George was already on his feet and approaching Alison sat beside Simon on the gargantuan settee. He bent over and kissed her gently on the cheek – "It's wonderful news, my dear," he said softly, "and I really cannot express just how happy I am for you both."

"Thanks, Dad," replied his daughter. The words were but a brace yet they were spoken with an emotion he had never known before in his daughter. Indeed, he felt closer to her at this moment than he had ever before during his life, and he had the conviction she felt likewise. Alison suddenly laughed, a nervous rather embarrassed giggle; "I really do not know how Heather knew I am pregnant – I'm not showing it yet, am I?"

"Oh yes you are," replied the farmer's wife, "you're showing it in your face. When I saw you at the kitchen door, I only had to catch a glimpse of your face to know you are pregnant. There is such an expression of fulfilment on it – and such an aura of contentment, and yet excitement, comes from you that there can only be one cause – and it does not need Sherlock Holmes to detect what it is."

"I never realised it," George interjected. "I never dreamt such a thing until you said just now.

"Well, you're a man," replied his wife simply, as if that was adequate explanation.

"So was Sherlock Holmes," retorted the farmer, though he was not sure such a statement had any relevance to the conversation.

"You must be absolutely delighted, Simon," cried Heather, bringing the silent rather brooding fourth member of the group into a conversation he had taken so little part in.

"Oh yes – yes indeed, Heather," he agreed dutifully. "We've always wanted a child – children in fact – but got to the state when we felt we would never have any. After all, we've been married some seven years now – which is quite a while. But it appears to be happening at last, and if all goes well, next May we will be parents. It's just that . . ." he stopped suddenly obviously confused and more than a little embarrassed – then promptly continued, "well, no, I don't really mean that; there cannot be a wrong time to have a baby when we want one so much. It's just that . . ."

"It's just that Simon has been made redundant," stated his wife, coming to the aid of a husband obviously unable to state with clarity feelings and thoughts which were not totally clear to himself. "He has worked for this company as a quantity surveyor ever since he left university more than ten years ago and thought his future there was assured. In fact, less than six months ago there was talk of him being promoted to being in charge of his section. Then, suddenly, almost overnight, the company was bought out by a huge national one."

"Surely they will need men of Simon's calibre," interjected an anxious George.

"No – they are totally 'changing tack' as they put it. Simon's entire section is being closed down and there are no jobs on offer within the company for any of them; so they all have to go."

"And the way everything is at present, my chance of getting another job in my field is remote to the point of being impossible," said Simon, his voice flat in its dejection. "And I do not have the qualifications to get anything outside my field, of course. No the future does not look bright, I'm afraid – although it should, with the baby coming. And that's what I really resent," he rasped, emotion – anger – in his voice for the first time. "This should be the happiest time of our married life – something we've both wanted all these years we've been together – and it's being ruined by these . . . these . . . these bastards who allow their accountants to ruin people's lives."

"Heavens, Simon, our lives are not being ruined," snapped his wife, "it's just that it has made life a little more difficult and complicated than we had anticipated. Fortunately I'm still in full-time teaching, and I shall be able to get maternity leave on full pay." She paused, looked at her husband – and received a slight nod from him.

"However, that's only the short term; obviously we have to look a bit further to the future – especially with an increase in the family due," she continued. "Obviously, I can continue to teach if I want – go back to work a few months after the baby is born. My job is probably reasonably safe for the foreseeable future, though with falling school numbers and so on, nothing is certain these days – and things have changed so much in education that there's

104

precious little joy in it all now. For Simon, though, the future is very bleak – and we both know it. He has been trying to get another job, naturally, but as he said just now, chances are not great. And even if he does, who knows how long before there would be another 'rationalisation' – as they call it – in terms of staff. The only alternative is to have a total change of direction – indeed, a complete change in our way of life. We've talked about it at great length over the past few weeks and we are agreed on the way forward."

She paused and glanced again at her husband seemingly hoping he would make a contribution to what she was saying, but he merely gave a brief shake of his head making it apparent that he would leave most of the talking to his wife. Briefly, she looked annoyed, but that expression moved away rapidly to be replaced by a look of earnestness, as she gazed firstly at Heather then at her father.

"Heather, Dad – what I am going to say now might well appear to you to be quite appallingly presumptuous – and far worse. It might appear to be a totally unwarranted, even unforgivable intrusion into your private affairs and business. I will say here and now it is not intended to be; it is merely the thinking out loud of two people who are up against it just a bit but who can see a possible solution which would not only benefit them, but which, hopefully, could benefit you as well."

George nodded, then glanced at his wife – whose face registered no emotion. "Carry on, Alison," said he, softly.

"I'm sure Simon will agree with me when I say that even before this whole series of events overtook us – the positive one of my being pregnant and the negatives of him losing his job without any good chance of getting another and of me becoming increasingly disenchanted with mine – we were seriously thinking of leaving Brighton and the south-east. You'll appreciate the reasons, Dad – after all, you did it. The pace of life, the stress of it all, the pressures, the feeling that you have perpetually to keep running, metaphorically, just to keep up – we have both long since had enough of it and both wanted to get out. I've so often thought of those lovely holidays we used to have down here in Devon when we were kids, whilst Simon had an uncle and aunt – now dead – who used to farm in North Devon, near Bideford, and for many years he would spend part of his summer school holidays staying there with them. He enjoyed every minute of it, and we often in recent years have talked of throwing up everything and moving down to the South West – just like you did. Oh, I know it was different with you as you were retired, but it seemed that if we waited till we retired we could well have died in the meantime. And you moving down here, then eventually going farming with Heather, really made us think very seriously about ripping up our roots and replanting them in Devon soil." She stopped once more, and laughed, rather nervously. "You must wonder when on earth I am ever going to come to the point; well, I'll come to it now, with a vengeance. In the letter you sent us a couple of months back, Heather, you wrote that your brother was about to go to Canada – probably permanently – and that you would miss him greatly, obviously in the personal sense and also because he was a vital member of a small unit here and his going would put much pressure on everybody else. What you wrote set us thinking – very hard, and very deep. And we have come up with a proposal which, honestly, is staggeringly impertinent and brash but which might just appeal to you. Put simply, Dad – Heather – Simon and I would like to move away from Brighton and come west to Devon – and, more importantly, to Bray Barton. We have never been here before today, of course, but your description of it when you came to see us that day before you were married, was exceedingly accurate. You spoke of its beauty, you spoke of the space all around and you also said just how big the house is – 'large enough to billet a regiment of soldiers' is the way you put it, as I recall. Well, we've no ambitions to get you to put the army up here, but we would like very, very much to move here to Bray Barton to live – to help fill this lovely old, and big house. Not just as lodgers, I must emphasise; oh no, we would like to buy a share of the tenancy of the farm – I recall you saying Heather, that your family had been tenants here for generations, with the farm actually being owned by the Duchy of Cornwall. And Simon would wish to be a working partner – albeit junior, naturally. And I, hopefully, would be able to help in some way as well. I will confess that I know nothing about farming at all, whilst Simon's knowledge, though considerably greater than mine, owes more to the pages of a book than to any practical experience."

Her husband nodded his agreement as she said the words and

interjected, "And I well realise that hill farming around and on Dartmoor is a particular art – but one," he added quickly, "I would be desperately keen to master if you were agreeable to us coming here. Certainly, I have no illusions about it at all – and nor does Alison. It will be hard, often frustrating, but always challenging – which is what I need. Also, it will be different which is what I also need. Possibly most vital of all, our child – or, who knows, perhaps even children – will grow up in the fresh air, amidst trees and fields and those awesome moors out there. What a start for them in life, eh? Wonderful."

Simon's words were the most enthusiastic and optimistic the farmer had ever heard his son-in-law utter and he was about to tell him so, but his daughter spoke again before he was able to.

"So there it is – our plans for the future – unusual, radical and, no doubt, foolhardy to a degree, but believe it or not the result of a very long period of thought and discussion by both of us, which as you will know, is very much our way. I've never done anything in my life without careful thought, whilst Simon, of course, is as cautious a man as the world has ever seen. But our plans are of no relevance whatsoever, naturally, if they do not find favour with you two. This is your farm, and your home, and the decision is obviously yours entirely – and whatever it is, Simon and I will abide by it without further discussion or argument. Obviously you will need time to make it – though not too much time, hopefully – and no doubt you'll phone us when you have made it."

"Of course, of course," responded her father hastily. "Heather and I will give it serious thought and come back to you as soon as possible – won't we dear?"

His wife nodded, her face devoid of expression. "Yes – as soon as possible," she concurred in a soft, rather flat intonation.

"One thing I would like to say before we go on to talk of other things," said Alison, her tone apologetic, her face awash with contrition, "is that I am ashamed of the way I behaved that day you came to visit us before you were married. I was rude, selfish and inhospitable and it was unforgivable. Simon took me to task after you left – which is most unusual for him – and I said to him that I would write to you to apologise, but I never did get around to it. Well, I have got around to it now – at last. Heather, I am truly sorry I treated you in such a way; also, I will say that I was totally wrong about you becoming Dad's wife. I thought it would be a disaster when it's easy to see that it has been a triumph. I have never seen my father looking fitter or happier, which is marvellous. As for you, Dad, I hope that no matter what happens, whether we come here to live or not, we will all be closer in the future than we have been in the past. These last few weeks since I've known about my pregnancy, I've thought a very great deal about the relationship between parents and children and realised that whilst I was always close to Mum, there was never the bond between you and I there should have been — and I was mostly to blame for that."

"I reckon there was fault both sides, my dear," muttered her father, somewhat embarrassed.

"Whatever, Dad, I hope that from now on we can all share our lives just a little bit — for all our sakes."

George nodded, rather bemused — though genuinely moved — over his daughter's words. He floundered around in his own mind for a reply, but before he could say anything, his son-in-law had made a request. "It's a pleasant day, George; is it possible for us all to go outside and have a stroll — and perhaps see a bit of the farm. After all," he added, with a rare smile, "if we do eventually end up with a partnership in the place, we should have a look at what we are buying into."

"Yes — of course," agreed his father-in-law. "Good idea, Heather, don't you think?" He was anxious to involve his wife who seemed to have become ever more withdrawn as Alison had spoken of her hopes and plans for the future. What Heather thought and felt, of course, was an essential element in the entire matter. She had gone quiet, and become a little aloof from the rest, but George knew her well enough to know that such behaviour did not signify hurt, or anger, or alienation, or any such emotion. It meant, rather, that she was confronted by major issues and that her mind was dominated by them and would continue to be until she came to a decision. And as she led her guests and husband across the kitchen and out into the wide concrete yard, she was beginning the exhaustive process in her mind of arriving at one.

Chapter Thirteen

It was more than a month before Heather Tennant arrived at her decision regarding her step daughter and son-in-law's request to buy into, and live at, Bray Barton. Technically the decision, and the arriving at it was a joint effort involving both she and her husband, but whilst he was happy to put his own views and feelings forward, he knew that the deciding of whether or not radical and, probably, irreversible change came to the farm, had to lay with her.

For Heather's forbears had trod those bleak acres for generations and he knew that her principle ambitions were dynastic – that her progeny would farm Bray Barton when she was gone and their issue likewise. That was why she was so desperate for a son; she had stayed home and farmed with her father but Nicola might well pursue another career or marry and follow her husband into a different way of life – daughters usually did. A son, though, could well decide that his future lay in the soil from which he had sprung and whilst his surname would not be Maunder, there would most assuredly be Maunder blood in his veins – and the line would remain unbroken in terms of farming at Bray Barton.

Heather approached the matter in as practical a manner as was possible, trying hard to leave out personality, personal desire or prejudice. Mentally she lined up the pros and cons, found that the pros were in the majority, dwelt on that fact for a while, then, over breakfast one drizzly, raw November morning, after Frank Morton and Phil Miller had just vacated the kitchen following consumption of coffee and biscuits – the routine if they were working in, or around the yard – plainly made her decision known to her husband; still, seeing as they had discussed most of the issues involved over a period of weeks, he was aware of what she was going to say.

She for her part realised that George had stood back deliberately to leave her to decide the future of Bray Barton, and of his daughter and husband, and appreciated the reason for it. And she felt his considerate attitude, whilst typical of him, was also the right one. For Bray Barton belonged to her family not to George's and whilst the man she loved was now a member of that family, his children were not, and never could be. So although he was involved in the decision making, the final say was hers — a situation she would have demanded had it not already been conceded.

She poured another cup of coffee for herself and her husband, put them down on the kitchen table and sat down opposite him. "I got through to Derek in Canada last evening George — whilst you were down at the pub. Bit of a caper actually — I got the wrong number the first time. Still, I got through to him in the end and we had a good discussion — and a long one. I shudder to think what our phone bill will be."

"They're well?"

"Oh yes, fine. Settling in well but somewhat overwhelmed with the country at present. Such a different way of life for them. Anyway, I put our suggestions to him and he was fully in favour — delighted, in fact. I fancy a sizeable cheque coming his way at the present time will be most welcome; I know he said before he went that they were all right financially in the short term, but Derek was always prone to understate things. If truth be known, they are probably finding things quite tight money-wise at the moment."

"So what do we tell Alison and Simon?"

"Well, as we agreed George, in principle they are welcome to buy into Bray Barton — and to come here to live. Most certainly this house is plenty large enough to accommodate another family — and, with a few small alterations, they can live entirely separately from us. The important thing, of course, is the financial side of it all — and their percentage holding. We have gone into this very thoroughly, George, haven't we — and consulted our solicitor; so we are clear on the way forward now that we have made a positive decision. There can be no negotiation on the principle — or on the percentage division in terms of the

110

partnership, though the final actual cash amounts will have to be settled by all the solicitors involved, including the fellow acting for Derek. You do agree George, don't you?"

"Yes, my dear, I do – entirely." And he did. For the proposals Heather was about to put to Alison and Simon were both fair and logical for all concerned, though the Brighton based couple would most certainly not be getting a bargain. Where land and property was concerned, Heather Tennant was no soft touch; rather, the blood of generations of tough hill farming folk coursed her veins – men and women who had grafted, fought and slogged for every penny, and for every square yard of their land. She, like them, knew the importance of both and would not bequeath a bargain to anybody – even her dear husband's kith and kin.

"So let's run through the figures again. You've no doubt got them fixed in your mind, but I'm still a touch hazy."

"Well," she continued, "at present we hold fifty-one per cent of the tenancy, with Derek holding forty-nine per cent. It used to be fifty, fifty, of course, but we suggested to Derek before he left that we buy one per cent of his share so that we had the controlling interest in Bray Barton – vital, obviously. After all, we have to be in a position to make major decisions and we couldn't do that if we had to consult Derek, thousands of miles away, on such matters. So on the phone last night it was vital to get his agreement to sell part of his share to Alison and Simon. He most definitely did not wish to sell all of it – there's a strong streak of caution in Derek; he no doubt wishes to keep alive the option of returning to Bray Barton should things fail to work out for them over there. Still, I fancy the time will come when he'll be quite happy to sell his entire holding, but it could be a year or two, or more, before that happens. As it is he will keep a twenty-five per cent interest in the place, therefore selling twenty-four per cent to Alison and Simon. On top of that, they will have to pay us a lump sum, to be negotiated. After all, they will be occupying a goodly portion of the house once they've bought their share of the tenancy, and will have to pay no mortgage or anything like that. I wouldn't think they'll have any problems in that direction would you?"

"No – none at all," agreed her husband. "Simon will get a redundancy pay-off and there will be a sizeable sum to come from the sale of the house. And if it's a few months before they actually sell and move down here, she will be able to remain in her teaching job until she qualifies for maternity leave – or so she says, at any rate. So she'll be paid for several months even if she never actually goes back to teaching. No, I fancy money will not be one of their problems. The way of life, though, and the rigours of a Dartmoor farm – that's a very different matter indeed. I'm not at all sure they know what they are letting themselves in for."

Whilst George Tennant had doubts over the wisdom of his daughter and son-in-law coming west to farm, the couple themselves appeared to have none at all. They accepted the legal terms offered by their father and step-mother without hesitation in terms of their share in Bray Barton and, through their solicitor, soon agreed the financial side also.

It was, though, a further six months before the couple actually left Brighton for Bray Barton, the sale of their house taking longer than they had anticipated. So it was on a blazing day in late June that Alison and Simon Jenkinson, plus a baby son, Robert Simon, born on the first day of May, moved west to a new home and a very different way of life. Alison, technically, was still on maternity leave from her school – thus on full pay – and would remain so for as long as possible. There was no way, however, she would ever return to teaching in Sussex so the monthly pay cheque would soon cease. She had not ruled out trying to obtain a teaching job in Devon, however, when Robert got past the baby state – possibly on a part-time or supply basis. All that was to the future, though; the immediate mission was for them both to settle into a way of life which was almost as alien to them as would be existence on the moon.

Alison, however, settled to rural Devonshire life much more rapidly than either she, or a rather sceptical father, had ever thought possible. A determined, single-minded woman when she wanted to be, she set about turning her share of the draughty, large-roomed farmhouse – a part of which had not been used since Arthur Maunder's death – into a comfortable home. The spending of some money and a fair bit of hard work, including wide ranging wielding of a paint brush and a goodly amount of wallpapering, plus some imagination and vision, had the place very comfortable by the time of Tavistock Goose Fair in October – an event she and Simon were to experience for the first time; and to find remarkably stimulating, despite the crowds, the noise, the smell and the tawdriness of some of it. By the time the Christmas holly was put about the place, Alison had her new home looking like a show home.

The two families had a good yuletide, spending parts of it together, but not overburdening each other with their company. The highlight, naturally, was dinner on Christmas Day. They all gathered in the huge, little-used dining-room at Bray Barton, to gorge of a feast prepared by Heather. And when they had just about finished the superb meal, George walked around the table and topped up the glasses – then glanced at his wife, a somewhat embarrassed grin on his face. Heather took her cue. She pulled herself to her feet, picked up her glass and held it high; "Could I ask you all to raise your glasses in a toast to the next Tennant – a boy, of that I am confident, name as yet unchosen, who will be born some time next July – probably." For a few seconds Alison and Simon were nonplussed – then realisation of what Heather was saying engulfed them, and they responded with a chorus of 'congratulations' and 'marvellous news' and so on. The glasses were indeed raised and their contents emptied – then filled again.

"You must be so pleased, Heather," commented her daughter-in-law. "I know you always wanted a second child."

"No business having another, really," said George Tennant, a serious and concerned expression upon his face. "The doctors are against it – all of them," he added vaguely. "Could badly affect her health – even put her life in danger. But she would not listen."

"She's the cat's mother," replied his wife spiritedly. "I – I have listened, but I do desperately want us to have a second child, hopefully a son – a farmer always should have at least one son – but if it's a daughter we will cherish her as a wonderful sister to Nicola. There is some small danger, yes, and it's a fact that doctors did advise me not to have more children, and George certainly wished to abide by that advice. But I do feel it's not fair for any child to be a single one if it can possibly be avoided. Having said that, though, I have given in to George now and agreed that after the birth of our baby, whether it be boy or girl, I will agree to them doing to me whatever it is they do so that I cannot have any more children." She giggled. "So these feast days are safe from now on when it comes to me imparting news about babies. News of Nicola's impending arrival was given to the throng at the dinner table on Easter Sunday and now I've chosen the most famous birthday of all to spread the tidings this time."

"And glad tidings they are," cried Simon raising his glass once again, then drinking deeply from it. He was certainly in good spirits, and unusually ebullient – and it was good to see him so, mused his father-in-law. For he had been a little concerned about the rookie farmer since his move to Bray Barton back in the summer. Not that there was any lack of effort from his son-in-law; the contrary, in fact. For Simon, disillusioned with his chosen profession long before he had been made redundant, took that dismissal as being a sign that he was meant to tread a far different path. Such a path could not have been more alien to his knowledge, experience and previous way of life, than hill farming on Dartmoor, but he was determined to make a success of it. Indeed, he had to. A large part of his and Alison's capital after the sale of their home in Brighton and his quite small redundancy payment had been used to pay off their mortgage and buy into Bray Barton, and there was but a modest amount remaining.

Thus did Simon fight to integrate himself into the ways of farming upon thin soil at Bray Barton. He found it hard. Not essentially a practical man, he had no natural way with either machinery or animals, nor, unfortunately, no real feel for the land at all. Also, he found the Devonshire weather trying – far more rain than sun at most times, and with the onset of winter, a constant raw, wet, often biting wind. Indeed, as he had remarked to Alison many times during the weeks leading up to Christmas, when working outdoors – where, inevitably, most of the work on a farm lay – he was rarely dry, and never warm.

And he was to say the same thing during the long, dark, cold, damp, often snowy months which followed Christmas, through the constant round of feeding and checking stock and sheep, mucking out cattle pens, labouring for Frank Morton – highly skilled in the old country crafts – as he set about repairing gaps in the grass and moss laden hedges on the lower part of the farm with stone, bedded into earth, whilst on the higher reaches adjoining the moor, building up the dry stone walls which carried no foliage at all. This was done not so much that Bray Barton stock be kept on the farm – they legitimately spent a large part of the year up on the moors, especially in spring and summer – but to ensure that animals up on the wild plateau which belonged to other farmers were not able to drop in on Bray's well-fed acres during the leaner months of the year, to fill their bellies at the expense of Heather and George's stock.

This was cold, finger-numbing work – slow, boring, repetitive – especially if denied the creative and skilled part of actually laying the stones into place. Yet Simon stuck to the work in a way which gained the admiration of his tutor. In fact nightly in the village pub Frank would regale his drinking companions with tales of the rookie's progress – or lack of it as the case might be. Indeed, ever since before George had married Heather and become involved deeply with the farming of Bray Barton, there had been a spotlight of curiosity – and an ever primed penchant for mirth – concerning the actions of the 'townies' who knew nothing about the land. For these were folk who had, generally, farmed in the area for generations, tough, proud, knowledgeable men who took their profession, and way of life, seriously. They critically doubted the ability of those from outside the area – and certainly from an urban background – to be able to master the myriad skills essential to the hill farmer, and to be able to handle the ever-uncertain, and occasionally malevolent climate.

In the past couple of years, as George had come to terms slowly with his new craft – if not actually fully mastering it – the spotlight on Bray Barton had dimmed somewhat, but with the coming of Simon and Alison, the full power had been switched on once again. Frank Morton, however, was a very fair man, and whilst he did not hesitate to tell of Simon's naïvity in farming matters, he was not slow to praise the fellow either. "Not afraid of work, I'll give him that," he would say between sips from his pint. "And he never complains about the weather either, even though I can see he's half dead with the cold and wet. And he really is getting the hang of hedging, at last; and a lot of other work as well. He hasn't a clue when it comes to milking, mind you, but he's starting to get a bit of a feel for stock – you know what I mean." And they did know his meaning exactly – that Simon could now sense if an animal was unwell, if stock needed more fodder or moving to a field which afforded them better shelter from foul weather.

And when the lambing season came, towards the end of March, Simon acquitted himself very well indeed. He worked the excessively long hours vital during the six to eight week period, learnt quite quickly, was dedicated and conscientious and, he had to admit to himself, despite the seemingly ever present rain, and the drudgery involved in it all, found the entire business of supervising new life coming into the world extremely fulfilling and stimulating. In fact the birth of hundreds of young lambs induced a birth in himself – that of self-confidence. By the end of April, for the first time since he had begun farming the previous summer, he felt that perhaps there was a future for him on the land – perhaps he could master it all and gain the respect of the professionals he worked with, especially the likes of Frank, Phil Miller and, most important of all, his young stepmother, Heather Tennant.

Certainly it was something of a relief to Heather and George, as summer approached, that Simon was able to play an ever greater role in the running of Bray Barton. For Heather's pregnancy was becoming as difficult and fraught as doctors and gynaecologists had predicted it would be. She was regularly in and out of hospital – sometimes staying for several days – for tests, observation and treatment for a multitude of ailments which, left unchecked, could have threatened she and her baby alike.

These ongoing problems, escalating as she edged ever closer to the baby's projected birth date, dominated the Tennants' lives – especially George. For whilst, obviously, it was Heather who was physically afflicted by all the myriad problems of a complex pregnancy, it was her husband who did the bulk of the worrying. He was heard to say, often, that he was 'far too old for this game,' and, now past his middle fifties, he probably was. Heather, though, was as sanguine as ever. Despite all the problems her body kept throwing up, all the barriers to a safe and successful birth, she remained single-mindedly certain that all would be well – in the end. And it was. For on July 25th, a day of thunder, lightning, often lashing rain – a day when 'the Gods are on the move', as Simon put it in poetic parlance – Heather was delivered, once again by Caesarean section, of a boy, to be named Adrian George. A mere sprat of a lad he weighed in at under five pounds, but he was, nonetheless, fit and strong as was his mother after the birth.

"Amazing – absolutely amazing, Mr Tennant," remarked the obstetrician to George less than an hour after the birth. "We have been extremely worried about your wife – a fact of which you are well aware, of course. And we had reason to be – there were so many problems Mr Tennant. Yet, at the end, it's all gone remarkably well. A woman of rare strength is Mrs Tennant – in both body and spirit."

"Oh yes, doctor – indeed she is." The farmer did not need to be told that – though compliments directed at Heather always pleased him.

"There can be no question of further children, of course," continued the doctor, rather gravely. "But then, you both know that – and, of course, agreed we ensured that Mrs Tennant is unable to conceive further."

George nodded. "There's no argument at all from me on that score, doctor – and Heather accepts it, though only with a measure of reluctance. She is essentially the most practical and realistic of people, however, and she knows that to have any more children could well prove fatal for her."

"Not 'could well', Mr Tennant," replied the doctor in tones which registered no uncertainty. "Rather, most assuredly would."

They were words which confirmed, for all time, the correctness of the mutual decision of husband and wife that Heather be rendered incapable of bearing further children – as far as George was concerned, at any rate.

What was important now was that the Tennants had a 'pigeon pair' of girl and boy – and that the Maunder 'dynasty' and 'succession' at Bray Barton appeared to be assured. In fact, there were almost enough 'young kids' at the farm 'to start up their own nursery school' according to Phil Miller; something of an exaggeration, of course, but with three children in the house under the age of three, young blood most assuredly abounded – as did the noise of washing machines, and the crying of children wishing to be changed or fed, or both.

Yet the two households rapidly settled into a pattern, with Heather soon gently organising her brace of young offspring into her daily routine, which still included some work on the farm, whilst Alison, who during parts of her young mother-in-law's fraught pregnancy had taken care of Nicola, now reverted to caring for Simon and young Robert, and augmented their income by marking exam papers of mature students at the Tavistock Community College. So life at Bray Barton, by and large, was settling down to a regular, though by no means dull, routine.

117

Chapter Fourteen

It was a scream which would haunt George Tennant for all of his life. He was walking across the yard at the back of the farmhouse towards the loose-box which housed a sick steer on a windy, but relatively mild day in mid-November, when it rent the air; it came from a bedroom at the back of the house – and it was made by Heather. How he knew that he did not really know; he had never heard her scream before, and Alison was also in the house – but it was Heather, of this there could be no doubt. The farmer swung around instantly and ran towards the kitchen door as fast as his ageing legs would take him. He stumbled into the kitchen, through it to the door on the far side, slightly ajar, thrust it open then ran through into the large hallway beyond and began to scale the stairs, two at a time.

Looking upwards, he saw Heather standing at the top gazing straight ahead, her face ashen, but registering absolutely no emotion; indeed, she stood frozen, almost statuesque.

"What is it, Heather – what's happened?" They were questions which tumbled from his lips but to which, in his heart, he knew he did not really want an answer.

His wife glanced at him then looked away again – straight ahead, unblinkingly at the far wall. "It's Adrian; it's our darling little Adrian. I believe he's dead."

The words lanced George Tennant like arrows shot from a bow. For just a couple of seconds he stood immobile gazing at his wife; she had to be wrong – the baby was asleep, nothing more than that, surely. But this was Heather talking – Heather, a woman never given to histrionics, drama, even overstatement. Cold, numbing fear gripped him as he stumbled forward towards their bedroom where lay the baby's cot, his mind dominated by that sole fact – this was Heather talking.

He went into the room and approached the crib, slowly, as if terrified at what he was about to see – which, indeed, he was. He gazed down upon the tiny body of his infant son, and knew instantly that 'body' it was. He had seen death before, many times, though never before in a baby – and he was only too aware that Adrian Tennant was dead, having lived in this world for fewer than four months.

Doctor Conway diagnosed the tiny lad's passing as being the mysterious 'cot death'. Certainly there was no obvious other cause, with Adrian having appeared to be, throughout the many and constant checks which babies receive, a healthy normal child. The medical man himself was most shocked, only ever having come across one previous similar case during all his long years of practice. Also he was concerned about the parents – especially Heather. For a man of George's age to be confronted with such a tragedy made him a medical risk, especially as he remained an epileptic, the general absence of fits due solely to the medication he took every day. But he was a tough, resilient man, and the doctor felt he would probably come through it all with the inevitable scars healing sufficiently not to pose a permanent threat to his health. Heather, though, was very different. She too was resilient, of course, and a woman of enormous strength of character. But she had just lost the baby boy for whom she had endured nine months of discomfort, often pain, occasionally distress, to bring into the world. She had lost the son and heir to Bray Barton she had almost been created to deliver – or so she saw it. And – a dreadful relevance which was not lost on Doctor Conway – the medical profession had ensured she could never conceive another child. Visiting Bray Barton every day for the first fortnight after Adrian's death – a period which included the deeply distressing funeral, with the mourners following behind a coffin smaller than a window box – the medical man became deeply worried about Heather, and voiced his concern to her husband.

"I feel given time and understanding, Heather will recover from the baby's death," he opined in considered tones. "But it will not be quick, George. In fact it could take months for the deep depression which has engulfed her to leave her be – perhaps even years; that's the worst scenario."

"I didn't realise she was anywhere as depressed as you say she is."

"Since the death, she has had to keep going physically, and, to a degree, mentally," he replied. "Death creates activity – in the short term. People coming to give condolences and so on, often folk you've not seen for quite a while, such as your son from Guildford – Martin, isn't it – and his wife who have come down to stay for a few days. And there's the funeral itself, of course – a traumatic time, but a busy one as well. But soon all will be quiet – all will be routine. And you face long winter months – the darkness of long winter nights, and the dourness of the days, and the cold and damp of the weather. Not the best of times if you are in good spirits – dreadful days if you are very down. And take it from me, Heather is as low, I do believe, as any woman can get."

"I did not realise," muttered her husband.

"No need to blame yourself for that, George – though you must have noticed that, quite obviously, she's not been herself since the tragedy."

"Well, no – obviously not. But then, nor have any of us. Naturally it will have hit Heather more than anybody else – she was the poor little mite's mother for heaven's sake. But surely, as time passes, she'll come to terms with it – don't you think?" George Tennant had a dread increasingly taking hold of him that Doctor Conway viewed Heather's journey back to relative mental normality with a very great deal of pessimism.

"Hopefully, George – in time. I shall, of course, call regularly to see her. In fact, I shall call often and unbidden – with, I trust, your blessing."

"Yes, naturally," agreed the farmer instantly.

"My hope is that I am able to help her with both words and medication. As a student doctor, I did quite an in-depth study of depression and general mental problems, and to a degree, it has stood me in good stead over the years. I'm not a consultant you understand – not what could, in medical terms be described as an expert. But I know the field fairly well, and if I'm honest, I enjoy that type of medicine – very fulfilling. And I do truly believe I can return Heather very largely to her old self – though such a tragedy will leave scars which never will be fully healed."

The farmer nodded his agreement, and was about to voice his thanks to this doctor who had been such a good friend to them over the years, when he found himself once again on the receiving end of words of wisdom – and a warning.

"What you must realise George – and it's not easy to say this, and most certainly exceedingly difficult to explain – is that, assuredly in the short term if not longer, you and your presence could well be a cause of Heather's depression rather than a cure for it."

The farmer shook his head in bewilderment; "You've lost me," he muttered.

"The plain fact is George – and one I foresaw soon after I confirmed that little Adrian was dead – is that Heather, although not blaming you in any way for his death, obviously not, is going to hold you responsible for the situation whereby she is unable to conceive another child."

"But that was a joint decision, doctor – you know that. You, and every single consultant and doctor we ever saw did not even want her to have Adrian because of the danger to her health – her life in fact. And when she insisted on having another baby because of her – well, virtual obsession regarding having a son, you were adamant that she be rendered medically incapable of ever having another child, and we both went along with that, she almost as readily as me."

"Quite so," agreed Conway. "But she went along with it then because she was already pregnant, and she was convinced she was going to have a son – which, of course, she did. And if that boy had lived then she would have been perfectly happy with the size of her family. But Adrian is dead; she now has no son, and she partly blames we doctors for that situation but she mainly holds you responsible for allowing the consultant to sterilise her – which is what it amounts to. Reason, logic, fairness do not come into it George, I'm afraid."

"How do you know this?"

"Because she's told me so. Oh, I have to admit that I searched for it in her a few days ago when I prescribed a strong anti-depressant drug to help her get through things in the short term. She talked – and rightly and healthily – of Adrian, of what a lovely baby he was and what a wonderful boy and man he would have become. Then her tone and attitude changed suddenly – and she spoke with great bitterness over the fact she could never have another child. Instantly I gave her the facts that her health could

f

not have stood up under a further pregnancy – indeed, her life would have been threatened by such. And I further tried to draw the poison by saying that nobody was to blame for such a situation; I pointed out that the decision had been a joint one made by herself and you, taking the very strong advice from the consultants and me. For some reason she seems unwilling to blame me in any way – perhaps because I have known her all of her life. But she does blame the consultants and she does blame you, saying you were in collusion with them, saying that she never wanted to be made sterile and that she only agreed to it at a moment of great weakness – literally that, because of the fraught pregnancy she endured."

"My God – I never dreamt she felt like that."

"Well, as I said just now, there has been too much going on for her to concentrate on her grief and her obsessions. But it will come, George – and very soon now. And, sadly, you will bear the brunt. I will help as much as I possibly can, with medication – and more importantly, with counselling. But it's you towards whom her anger and resentment will be directed, and it will not be easy to live with. But live with it you must if she is to recover – and your marriage is to survive. Although she does not know it, she needs you now more than she ever has. In fact, with her remarkable resilience and self containment, this could be the very first time she has ever really needed you; come to that, it could be the first time in her entire independent life she has ever needed anybody."

Doctor Conway's diagnosis of Heather, and his predictions as to her subsequent behaviour were accurate to a degree which was quite remarkable. For the farmer's wife's depression really took hold when life at Bray Barton resumed to something approaching normality, whilst her anger and resentment at never again being able to bear a child were directed in full force against the hapless George. Indeed, so far did it go that he was virtually cut out of her life.

Nicola was still warmed by what love and affection emerged from Heather, whilst their stepmother continued to treat Alison and Simon with courtesy, albeit often cold and remote. And Frank Morton and Phil Miller were still accorded the basic respect they had always received from Heather – although they rarely saw her throughout the winter days, she no longer appearing to take any active interest in the running of the farm, and when they did they found her sad, unsmiling and rather uncommunicative.

Poor George, though, felt a total stranger to her. She spoke to him on occasions – but never seemingly unless she had to regarding some practical matter – and she cooked his meals, though she often found excuses not to share meal-times with him. About a week after Doctor Conway's warning regarding her behaviour she stopped sleeping with her husband, making the excuse that Nicola had a nasty cold so she wanted to share her room at night to ensure the little girl was not lonely or frightened if she had a coughing spasm during the long nights; and when she moved out of the bedroom, George knew she would not be back. Nor did she return.

A bleak Christmas passed – the worst the farmer had ever known – to be followed by long, cold weeks during which life for him was scarce worth the living. Doctor Conway was a regular visitor to Bray Barton and a most sympathetic ear as far as George Tennant was concerned, but despite valiant efforts, he was unable to improve matters even fractionally. Indeed, in moments of contemplation he admitted to himself – though never to her husband – that Heather's condition was worse than he had anticipated it would be; so bad, in fact, he felt there was real doubt as to whether she would ever recover – a sad, indeed dreadful prospect, for it would mean the total end of as loving and fulfilling a marriage as he had seen in many a year, and the ruination of the lives of a man and young woman for whom he held both respect and affection. As February moved into March he felt that everything he was doing was leading nowhere – that he really had to think along different lines. An old friend of his, an expert in mental disorder and depression, practising in Plymouth, came to the Conways for dinner one night and, after the fine meal, the GP picked his friend's brains.

"Well, I'll have to see her, of course," he said. "Can't diagnose mental problems over meat and veg no matter how good it is. It sounds to me like a very difficult case, though, I must say – no guarantee of bringing her back even with the most intensive treatment. We are, however, using a very different type of treatment for cases such as you describe. It involves some of the old electrical shock treatment – but a great deal more besides. Rather extreme, mind you, and only used when all other things fail."

"I really am afraid that all other measures will surely fail, old chap," replied Conway, gravely. "This special new shock business could prove to be the one remaining hope."

And he was right – though the shock treatment which came the way of Heather Tennant was very different from anything Doctor Conway and his consultant friend had in mind, but was to come her way within days.

For less than twenty-four hours after the dinner party at the Conways' house in Tavistock, the weather changed dramatically. For about ten days it had been cold, sharp frosty weather with the occasional flurry of snow; but through the night of Wednesday in the first week of March, the wind went to the north-east, rose, and snow began to fall along with the temperature. It became a foul night and edged slowly and dimly into a likewise day. George Tennant's spirits hit bottom as, whilst dressing, he gazed from his bedroom window at the crack of dawn – although he was so dispirited with life due to Heather's spurning of him, they did not have far to drop. One thing for sure, though, it was going to be the kind of day that would be judged a success if nightfall could be reached with all livestock fit, well and located in fields reasonably sheltered from the ferocious weather which was now hammering down upon them from the high moor.

He went down into the kitchen, put on the kettle – and was joined by Simon just as the large metal container boiled. George made a pot of strong tea, filled two beakers, placed them down on the large table and slumped down upon a hard kitchen chair.

"Well, it is not going to be an easy day, Simon. I've not known that many mornings like we've got today since I've been living in these parts, but when they do come it's got to be like living in the Yukon or some such place. Hellish."

His companion gazed through the window, then nodded – morosely. It was going to be one of those days when he questioned the wisdom of ever coming to this remote spot to try to wrest some sort of living from soil so thin it would scarce make mud, and a climate, at times, so cold and wet the sun appeared an illusion.

"I suppose we spend the day just feeding around, as we do most days this time of year – only more so," he muttered.

"That's well put, Simon. But there are extra problems, I'm afraid. To start with Frank Morton won't be here. As you know, his wife phoned in yesterday morning to say he was down with a bad about of 'flu – which, as we know, has been coming on for days. Anybody other than Frank would have taken to his bed days ago – but he, being the man he is, went on until he virtually dropped. One thing for certain, if he ventures out today in his state, they'll bury him. And I don't expect Phil Miller will be in for a while yet. Although he does not work for his father, of course, he still lives at home so he'll be helping his mother and father check and feed their stock before coming over here – they don't employ anybody, so they will value his presence in weather like this. So, it's down to us, Simon – for the time, at least."

His son-in-law nodded his agreement, drained his beaker, then pulled himself to his feet. "Right, what do you want me to do first – feed the stock in the yard?"

"No – not this morning, Simon. I'll have to get on with the milking, of course, with neither of the two workmen here, but I suggest, with the weather this bad and showing signs of getting worse that you go out to the Boulder Field and check the ewes out there. Hopefully they'll be all right, but I'm a little concerned. Most of them are due to lamb within the next three weeks and whilst that field is not too exposed it's only one field's width away from the moors – so things up there could be worse than we might imagine. I should take a small trailer of food with you – but I wouldn't take either of the dogs. In conditions like these, if the ewes get too frightened some of them could easily abort. I leave it to you, Simon. If conditions out there are really bad – and you feel there's a danger they might get buried in the snow, then bring them down to the paddock at the back of the covered yard; you'll have no trouble moving them – they'll follow the tractor and trailer with all that food aboard. But only bring them down if you really feel it necessary – there's already too many stock in that paddock. Anyway, it's up to you."

His son-in-law nodded once again, though none too pleased. He was still greener than spring grass when it came to this hill farming caper and did not welcome having major decisions of animal welfare left to his own judgement. Still, he reasoned, George had sufficient on his plate at that moment, one way and another, so he would do the older man's bidding without further ado. He put on an old, but heavy and serviceable overcoat, a scarf, a woolly bobble hat – which he invariably wore during these

125

winter days – his wellington boots, then finally a pair of thick gloves; he was ready for the elements, or, at least, was as ready as he ever would be. He went out into the biting wind, driving stinging snow horizontally into his face, and made for the tractor shed on the far side of the yard. The weather was assuredly foul, with the steady, though by no means heavy snowfall being carried on an Arctic blast. As yet, although there was a substantial amount of snow about, it was not an accumulation which would cause any immediate problems in terms of mobility of transport. What it would be like on the more elevated terrain of the Boulder Field, however, was a different matter; and what conditions would be like on the moor itself did not bear thinking about.

Simon clambered aboard the smallest of the tractors – the Massey Ferguson – which thankfully started quite easily, drove it outside the shed, coupled it to a small trailer which stood in the far corner of the yard, then drove to the big forage and root shed close to the shippens on the opposite side. Laboriously he loaded the trailer with turnips, mangolds – all of it freezing to the touch – and a few bales of hay. Then he again got aboard the rather aged tractor, guided it across to the narrow, rutted lane which entered the yard at its top side and began to follow it, slowly, up to the Boulder Field. He was relieved that the snow in the lane, whilst substantial – and increasing – was still nowhere near thick or deep enough to hamper the sturdy progress of the Massey Ferguson. It was most assuredly cold, though, and Simon almost prayed – though not quite, having long since decided the existence of God was most unlikely – that he would find the ewes fit and well, and not requiring moving or any attention other than the distribution of the supplies borne by the trailer. If that was the case, then he would be back at the farmhouse before too long, where Alison would have a good old traditional breakfast awaiting him – with as much hot coffee available as would be needed by then to thaw him out.

He drove laboriously up the lane, the cold seemingly intensifying by the yard; the snow, however, was becoming a little less heavy. If it stopped altogether, he mused, then potential crisis would soon revert to ordinary cold winter routine – albeit, exceptionally cold routine.

He drew the tractor abreast of the gate leading into Boulder Field, got down and shuffled through the ankle deep snow with the intention of opening it. A couple of yards from it, he stopped in his tracks – for it was already open, or ajar to be more accurate. Whoever had been last through there – and it could well have been himself when feeding the previous day – had not latched the gate properly. So it now stood about five feet open, and the tracks of sheeps' cloven hooves, still slightly visible despite the fresh snow falling, gave ample evidence that the rugged, teak tough Dartmoor ewes – ever difficult to enclose – had decided it was time for a move despite the dreadful weather. Their natural affinity to wilderness had directed their feet up the lane towards the open moor at the top of the lane, whilst the clarity of their tracks suggested that Simon had missed them, possibly, by little more than minutes.

He groaned and shook his head. His breakfast and hot coffee receded into the distance; those ewes, though tough little beasts, were heavy in lamb and would have to be rounded up and brought back down to the Boulder Field – looking less snow-bound than he had expected, and assuredly a tropical island compared with conditions on the open moor.

He pulled back the gate as far as he could, the rapidly freezing snow making it impossible to open the barrier totally, then got aboard the tractor and backed it a few yards back down the narrow lane so that it would form an impossible barrier to sheep which, if things went to plan, would soon be scurrying back down the lane from the moors, himself in pursuit. When almost upon the tractor and trailer, his theory was they would use the only possible outlet – through the open gate and into Boulder Field.

Simon thrust his frozen hands deep into his pockets and began to plod, so very slowly, into the full force of the bitter wind, the snow – though little now was actually falling from the sky – being whipped into a swirling maelstrom. Eventually, after what seemed hours, but which was little more than ten minutes, Simon emerged from the lane onto the moor – and, amazingly, saw the sheep immediately in front of him. The weather was such that even they with their small, uncomprehending minds, were seemingly rapidly coming to the conclusion that the place they had recently left was vastly preferable to the one at which they had just arrived.

Pulling his bobble cap down as far over his face as it would go to try to afford some protection from the Arctic wind, the reluctant shepherd skirted slowly and stumblingly around the edge of the rather bewildered flock. A few on the outside of the flock showed mild signs of moving away from him, but before any had actually taken such action, he was around on the moor side of the squat creatures, and with a series of raucous shouts had stampeded them back instantly the way they had come – down the snowy, icy lane towards the Boulder Field, where they would be given sufficient fodder to keep their stomachs full for two to three days.

Simon was about to follow them when the thought struck him that it was by no means certain that all the sheep had returned from whence they came. He had had no chance to count them, of course; that he would attempt to do when he got down to the field. But if a few – or just one or two – had straggled away from the flock in the appalling weather then now was the time to check. Any longish period of time up here in such conditions could do heavily pregnant ewes a deal of harm, despite their natural resilience to extreme winter weather. And if there were such stragglers up here it was better that he established the fact now when he was here rather than down in the field a little later which would necessitate a frozen return. Just over to his left he saw a pile of rocks pushing up into the turbulent sky-line – a jagged finger. It was probably some thirty feet high, but if he climbed to about just over halfway up where a flattish piece of rock formed a small natural platform, then he would be able to see a short distance in most directions and possibly espy stragglers – as in these conditions if any ewes had detached themselves from the flock they would not have had time to wander far.

He thrust his, by now, seemingly half frozen body forward into the wind and struggled through the swirling snow to the base of the rocks; then, laboriously and carefully, he began to climb them – slippery as marble under a coating of black ice – until he reached the flat spot he had espied earlier. He pulled himself upright upon the platform and peered out and about through the dire, dark, threatening weather. He could not see far, but what little distance his sight did lance gave no evidence of sheep occupying it. He was pleased. He had been confident from the start that he had caught up with the flock before any of the ewes had time to defect, and now he was virtually certain.

So, his duty done, he turned to climb down from his dangerous perch, his mind already on the hot food and drink Alison would have prepared for him when he arrived back at Bray Barton's warm house – which should not be long now.

Perhaps it was the vision of comfort not far to the future which temporarily eroded his awareness of the dangers of the present surrounding him high up on that sinister slab of granite. Whatever, he suddenly moved forward to the edge of the small platform at a pace which would have been reckless on a summer's day, but which, in conditions as bad as most Dartmoor winters can produce, was to prove lethal. For his right foot landed squarely on a patch of black ice – a powdering of snow upon it – and instantly he was hurtling over the edge and crashing the fifteen feet, or so, down onto the rocks below, head first. For a few seconds his head and body moved as he lay amongst that brutal granite – but he soon lapsed into unconsciousness, the deep gash in his head oozing blood out through the woollen strands of the bobble hat, which still clung tenaciously to his head, onto the rapidly solidifying snow about him.

Chapter Fifteen

It was his father-in-law who found Simon's body. Alison had become a little concerned when he had not come in for breakfast by ten o'clock – an hour past his normal time – and alarmed when eleven came and went without him appearing. George, with so little to bring him into the farmhouse these days – except for little Nicola – would often go virtually all morning without a break from his tasks; on this day, with so much to do and fewer than normal to do it, he found that necessity had kept him out and about the yard and buildings. Phil Miller had turned up at about half past ten, and George had immediately sent him in the opposite direction to Simon down to the lower fields of the farm to check and feed stock there. The farmer had become vaguely aware he had not seen Simon, but merely assumed his son-in-law was now engaged on the jobs he would normally be about on a winter's morning, after successfully attending to the sheep in the Boulder Field.

He was putting some hay into a rack for a ravenous bunch of yearlings when he looked up and saw Heather standing just inside the door of the shed. Her presence surprised – indeed, almost startled him. She was not a regular sight out in the cattle sheds these days and also she was dressed merely in the jumper and jeans she would normally wear about the house – no coat, hat or anything, even though she would have had to cross the yard to get there.

Something was wrong – and different. "George," said she softly, "Alison's worried about Simon – she's just come in to me. He's not come in for his breakfast – or for a drink – anything. And the time is gone half past eleven. He's been out since first thing – where did he go?"

For a few seconds her husband did not answer – the central question as to the whereabouts of Simon Jenkinson being briefly sidetracked by an awareness that there was something different about Heather; there was a concern, even a sense of urgency and purpose about her which he had feared, along with so many other things, had gone forever.

"He went out to the Boulder Field – to check and feed the ewes there; and to bring them down to the paddock if he felt there was a need. My God, that was hours ago Heather – four now, almost."

She stared at him – indeed, possibly past him – and her face registered a deep dread. Suddenly she came to life, displaying more animation and awareness than he had seen in her since Adrian's death. "You must go, George. You must go and find him. Something – terrible could have happened. It's bad enough down here today – up there in the Boulder Field it will be much worse, and on the moors it will be hellish. No reason why he should be on the moors, I know – but something might have made him go up there – they're not far from the Boulder Field. You must go – right now, George. You must go. Come over to the house and I'll get you some more clothes to put on – you'll need them up there."

So George had been despatched to find his son-in-law and after a longish search in conditions which, though still exceedingly bleak, were improving slightly – with the wind dropping a little and the snow ceasing – he found him lying in a crumpled heap at the base of the 'jagged finger', the snow about his head a dark red. Simon lay half frozen in the sub-zero temperature, life, quite obviously, having left his body.

George Tennant felt numb – with both cold and shock. The one thing of which he was certain, however, was that this was a time for doing rather than thinking; a time to rescue his son-in-law – albeit, too late – from this malevolent moor. Thus he went down the lane to where the tractor and trailer still stood, started it up; drove it into the Boulder Field, distributed the load to a receptive, if not grateful flock, then drove the powerful machine success-fully up through the snow and ice bound lane to the moors. He parked it as close to Simon's body as he could – but that represented a distance of some fifty yards away. He often thought afterwards of the pulling, semi-carrying and dragging of the leaden body of Simon Jenkinson from his place of death to the trailer, then the lifting aboard of his tragic cargo, and wondered always as to how he achieved it. Exceptional strength seemed to come to him – probably the strength of desperation. Whatever, he lay the corpse flat onto the back of the trailer, clambered aboard the tractor then directed it slowly down the rutted, frozen, snowy lane towards Bray Barton yard.

It was about one-thirty when the Massey Ferguson and trailer bearing the remains of Bray Barton's latest trainee farmer, spluttered and slid slowly across the yard to halt some twenty yards from the back door of the farmhouse. He alighted as quickly as his, by now, numb limbs would allow him, but his feet had no sooner touched the ground than he saw Heather, still clad only in jeans and jumper – albeit with wellington boots on – running from the back door. Obviously she had kept an almost constant vigil since he had gone in search of Simon some two hours earlier.

George suddenly appreciated what a horrific sight awaited her, with her step son-in-law laying on that icy trailer, his dead face a mask of frozen blood; thus, with an alacrity almost remarkable considering his debilitating coldness and weariness, not to mention his age, he pulled off his heavy overcoat and lay it quickly over the top part of Simon's body – including the head.

The overcoat draped the corpse just as Heather arrived at the side of the trailer. She stopped in her tracks, her face virtually emotionless. First she gazed at the sole cargo aboard the trailer, then at George – who stood just a few feet away from her, his head bowed, his mind trying hard to come to terms with the fresh calamity which had befallen them.

Heather at first was silent, but then came the soft sound of crying – to be followed by sobs which reverberated around her body like severe electric shocks. "Oh, George – George; what's happening to us? Why these terrible things? Why always death? Dad, then Adrian – now Simon. Why, George, why? Are we cursed? Do you think that's what it is – there's a curse on us?"

Her husband stepped forward and for the first time in many months, took his wife in his arms – and she did nothing to stop him.

"I've no answer, Heather – obviously not. It's fate – and a very malevolent one at that." He looked at his wife's face, mottled a florid colour by the coursing tears plus the searing wind, and said, simply, "I love you Heather – deeply, unendingly and more than

132

words can say."

"Yes, I know, George – I do know." She closed her eyes and buried her head into his shoulder for a few seconds. Then she looked up at him and softly said the words almost carried beyond hearing by the wind, "And I love you – as much now as the day we were married. And I can only ask you to forgive me for the way I have behaved since Adrian's death. It's like I've been dead myself – but suddenly seeing poor dear Simon lying there, it's come home to me just how alive I am, and how lucky I am to be so. Simon can never hold Alison again the way I can hold you – or cuddle Robert as I'm able to with Nicola. I am so lucky, so, so, lucky, George, and it's taken this terrible event for me to realise it. George, do say you will forgive me – please, please, it's so important to me. I've treated you like a stranger these past few months – like you've meant nothing to me. I'm appalled at the way I've behaved to the man I love. So please say you forgive me."

Her eyes held a look akin to terror, so desperate was she for her husband's forgiveness. Despite this, though, she did not receive it. He merely shook his head and said, a gentle smile playing around his lips, "Forgiveness does not come into it, Heather. The reality is simply that I thought I had lost you – but now you are restored to me again. I thank God for it – and ask for nothing more."

He turned his head and looked at the trailer's macabre load; then he gazed again at his wife. "I've got a visit to make, my love – and news to impart. I am about to bring grief to my daughter – and I would appreciate it so very much if you came with me. I fancy you will be of greater comfort to her than I ever could be."

Heather nodded her agreement to her husband's request, and taking his half frozen hand led him across the yard towards the door which led into Alison's part of the house. A marriage saved – a life lost, thus a marriage over. It had been at Bray Barton, a climactic day.

Chapter Sixteen

As George Tennant had always known, his daughter turned after her mother in virtually all ways. She resembled her greatly in looks, whilst in character she had the same sharpness of wit and tongue, the same grit and tenacity, the same stubborn determination to take a sword to grief and despondency.

Thus her receiving of the news of the death of her husband, and her subsequent coming to terms with it, were both faced with dignity and positive thought. She and Simon had always had a good marriage – one of mutual understanding, respect and love. But though she grieved, she refused to allow grief to be her master. The inquest – where a verdict of 'accidental death' was brought, the medical evidence being that whilst Simon had not fallen a great distance, he had struck rocks from such an angle as to cause his neck to be broken, though he had probably not died instantly – and the funeral, were traumatic occasions but Alison, whilst shedding tears, never really let go the tight rein she had placed upon her emotions.

George admired her greatly, but as always felt he had little to offer her in terms of support. Whether this was because she did not require it, or for the eternal reason that he was unable to articulate in word and deed the affection he felt for her, he knew not. The fact that Heather, who could usually break the reserve of the most aloof person, also failed to get fully on Alison's wavelength at that time, pointed to it being the former.

The widow was helped in her facing the future as a single parent by the way her and Simon's marriage had evolved. For she had always been the dominant one, the decision maker, the one with vision – the leader. Thus, now on her own, in practical terms she had just her son to work and plan for, rather than two as before. So when she missed her beloved Simon over the months which followed, she gritted her teeth and got on with her life – for the sake of Robert.

And the following September the major step she took to break back into the 'mainstream' of life, as she put it, was to get a part-time teaching job in a primary school in Tavistock. She worked only two days a week, but she enjoyed both the involvement and the regular income which the job brought, Simon having left her not as well provided for as both she and him would have hoped. During the days Alison was at school, Robert, now well into his third year, was cared for by Heather – a task she enjoyed and found fulfilling.

So it was that life at Bray Barton settled slowly back into routine for them all and by the time of the coming, and passing of the first anniversary of Adrian's death, there were few outward signs in anybody's behaviour or talk to betray the reality of the dreadful year the residents of the farm had known. George made but one comment on that sad day when his son's premature death was a year old – "I hope none of us here, or anywhere for that matter, ever suffer another year such as we have known," he muttered, tears in his eyes. His wife, her face showing little emotion, but her eyes transfixed by grief, said not a word.

The Christmas which followed was a quiet, but by no means sombre one. The presence of Nicola and Robert at Bray Barton forced sad memory to recede, its place taken by the warm, generous hope for the future that was the yuletide season. And the holiday period was helped by the weather, it being the mildest driest Christmas time for years, thus cutting back on the amount of feeding and general care which the stock and sheep required – their numbers slightly depleted due to George, realising that they faced winter without Simon's help, selling off more stock than normal during the autumn. This short term move boosted the bank balance and slightly reduced the work-load – but George and Heather knew that long term Bray Barton would have to be farmed to its full potential in such difficult financial times as was afflicting farming generally, if solid viability was to be attained. Decisions on such matters, however, were not pressing, and would certainly keep until spring arrived and another anniversary of grief – that of Simon's death – had passed.

The winter meandered on its long, dark way, but whilst it

became wetter, it remained unusually mild. And by the time the lambing season began, a dryish spell of weather had returned, making it, in terms of meteorology, a season of birth and renewal as good as Heather could ever recall.

And it was at this time, some fourteen months after her husbands death, that Alison took the first step towards renewing her own life – inevitably in grief induced limbo since Simon's passing. Not that it was a step which Heather and George knew anything about until a couple of months afterwards, hearing of it for the first time over a drink at the Peter Tavy Inn.

It had been a searingly hot day, the kind that only late June could produce and the evening remained warm and hazy, but with a gentle breeze from off the moor neutralising any oppressiveness. It was a good evening to walk the couple of miles to the pub for a pint, George had opined to his wife over tea – the kind of suggestion he made perhaps three times a summer – when the right weather, a sympathetic inclination and a lack of pressing farm work all came together in a powerful triumvirate. Heather, fancying a relaxing evening, had concurred in principle and when Alison agreed to look after Nicola – the least she could do seeing as Heather had 'baby sat' Robert half a dozen times during the previous month, his mother taking herself off to evening classes in Tavistock – principle became reality.

The nature of Alison's 'evening classes' became apparent to them both, however, as they sat outside the pub that evening, the sun setting red as blood behind the nearby tors. For they were joined at their rough hewn wooden table by 'Spider' Baldwin – so named because of his exceedingly long, and thin, arms and legs – who farmed Torcrest, a rough, windswept holding high up on the moor itself (as the name suggested), a couple of miles from Bray Barton.

A kind, helpful man who had been born into a hill farming family and had lived in the parish all his life, Spider had given George a good deal of helpful advice and hints concerning the complexities of successful farming in the foothills of Dartmoor, especially during the first couple of years when the former London businessman had confronted a totally alien way of life. Indeed, Baldwin was the only farmer of George's acquaintance who knew more about hill farming than Heather.

Spider sat down on the hard bench beside George, placed a

small tray onto the table and lifted from it vodka and lemon for Heather, a scotch for George and for himself his regular tipple, a pint of scrumpy. Their conversation was somewhat akin to the evening – gentle and relaxed, though many subjects were covered, Spider being a man full of rumour and gossip as well as being knowledgeable about subjects ranging from politics to football, from the chance of some good growing weather to the price of lambs.

The pleasant though rather desultory conversation meandered through the drinking of the round which Spider had bought and then on to span the one purchased by George. The thin man drained his glass with the air of a man who was about to make for home – and then informed his companions of such intent.

"Better be getting on – shearing tomorrow," said Spider with a wry smile. "Enjoy that no end; about as much fun as going to the dentist."

"George manages to avoid that, don't you dear," replied Heather, laughing. "He delegates."

"I do that," agreed her husband in positive tones. "One job I've never done – and I've no intention of starting now. Phil Miller does most of ours – enjoys it too, for some strange reason. Frank gives him a hand, but it's mostly Phil. And he's good as well – and very quick."

At mention of Miller's name, Spider Baldwin's face registered a quizzical expression. "Not seen him in here tonight," he observed. "He's here most evenings I'm told. In fact, he was in here with your Alison last night, George." The comment was made in conversational tones, but the couple from Bray Barton were both aware that their farming neighbour was awaiting their reaction to what was most surprising news.

"Alison wouldn't have been here last night, Spider – she was at an evening class at Tavistock College," he retorted – rather sharply, but with a touch of uncertainty in his voice. "Though I suppose she could have been here later in the evening; the class finishes about half past nine – or so I believe."

"It was before that – well before that," replied Baldwin. "She came in with Phil about eight – and they were still here when I left about a quarter to ten. Nothing unusual, mind you, she coming in with Phil. They must have been in here to my knowledge, about half a dozen times over the past six weeks."

For a few seconds there was a heavy silence, neither Heather nor her bemused husband really sure how to react to this illuminating – and astonishing – news. As always, Heather was the first to click her mind into gear. "Well – it'll do Alison good to get out a bit. It's well over a year since Simon died – she cannot mourn forever. She's got a life to live." The words were spoken in a spirited, almost acerbic tone – and Spider Baldwin realised that he had possibly spiced friendly chat with innuendo.

"Yes – yes – yes, quite so Heather," he agreed hastily. "Do her a power of good, as you say. And I reckon young Phil's good company – all about, he is; quick witted, as you'll know, him working for you."

"Oh yes, he is that," agreed the farmer's wife. "And good as gold really; fiery temper though."

"Temper of the devil when he's roused," retorted Baldwin instantly – then, feeling he had said too much, he made an attempt to retract. "Not that there's any vice in him, mind you – nothing nasty at all. He's just like his father really – in a paddy in seconds if things go wrong, but back to normal just as quickly. But then, there's scores of us like that, isn't there?"

"Quite so," she agreed softly.

"Well, I'd better be away, as I said just now. Take care Heather – and you George. See you both soon I hope." He acknowledged their somewhat muted farewells with a wave of the hand glad to escape to his Land Rover parked around the back of the pub, being aware that he had perhaps put some slight strain on his friendship with the Tennants due to his rather careless chatter.

As he disappeared around the corner of the old building, Heather looked across at her husband gazing down at the scarred table top. "It's time we were off, George," said she. "It's half past ten and I told Alison we would be home by eleven at the latest; and you know Nicola – she never seems to really get off to sleep until we are home. By the time we walk it, it'll be eleven at least."

Her husband nodded, then got up from his seat. He glanced across at his wife, a rather hurt expression on his face. "Why didn't she tell us, Heather – why didn't she mention she was going out with Phil Miller. If Spider Baldwin knows then probably half the parish knows as well. She should have told us."

"Why George – why should she tell us?" retorted his wife, sharply. "After all it's none of our business is it? Alison is a mature woman; in point of fact, she is older than me – and there doesn't seem to be too many about to fit that category these days," she added in an attempt at a feeble joke. "As you should know, George, Alison is a woman of intelligence, foresight and strength of character. She is not of an age or disposition to do anything foolish. If she's going out with Phil it's probably that she simply enjoys his company on occasions – he is, as Spider said, a pleasant, outgoing sort of man to be with."

"He's also years younger than her," grunted her husband.

"Not that many," she rasped. "Five at the most. And from you that really is rich, George. After all, it is, I believe, a fact that there are many years between you and me – about twenty-five, yet it's never affected our relationship, has it?"

"That's different," he retorted.

"How for heaven's sake?"

"Well . . . well, it just is."

"It's not, George, and you know it. Look dear, there is probably nothing between Alison and Phil Miller. It's probably a mere friendship. But if it is more than that – or if it develops into more than that – then so be it. Alison is a very attractive woman with a strong personality and considerable intelligence, while Phil Miller is an exceedingly good-looking young man – and take my word for it, he most certainly is – with a lively personality and mind and, very important, the heir one day to a quite decent farm. In fact, if rumours about his father's heart condition are true, then he could be master of Holly Park sooner rather than later. So whatever the truth of it all at present, and the outcome of it – if there be one – it seems to me there is absolutely nothing for you to worry about at all; am I not right?" She spoke the final four words with spirit, and George, confused in his mind though he was, knew there was nothing to be gained from arguing with her. And indeed she could be right; after all, Heather was usually right. So he merely nodded, smiled a touch bleakly, kissed her gently on the lips then, taking her hand in his, began the mainly uphill walk back to Bray Barton, his daughter's behaviour – and possible future – to the forefront of his mind.

Immediately on waking the following day, the future of Alison – and young Robert, naturally – became again the topic which dominated his thinking over matters of more immediate urgency in practical terms, such as whether or not the Well Field should be cut for hay that sunny morning, and whether he should enter any store bullocks for the main July market at Tavistock in a fortnight's time. He dressed and was soon down in the kitchen, a large mug of sweet tea in his hand – his eternal start to the day – leaving Heather upstairs seeing to Nicola.

To his surprise there was a knock at the door which led from Alison's part of the house – at seven o'clock, much earlier than she would normally be about. "Come in," he invited – and the door promptly opened to reveal his daughter, clad in a bright red dressing-gown, and looking somewhat careworn.

"Hello, my love; everything all right? Bit early for you, isn't it?"

"Yes it is, Dad," replied she, rather tersely. "It's just that I wanted a chat with you – on your own. Although there's nothing I want to talk to you about that Heather should not hear, perhaps it's best initially if we have a chat just between the two of us."

"Of course," he agreed, gently; it was apparent she was a little agitated. "Cup of tea?"

"Please."

He poured from the huge teapot, filled the largish mug almost to the top, added a splash of milk, then handed it to his daughter, who had sat down opposite him at the large kitchen table.

"Well, what do you wish to discuss, Alison. Something appears to be troubling you."

"I suspect you know, Dad – Heather as well. I'm not sure, of course, but when you came back from the pub last night, you were both just a little odd – you especially. It was as if you didn't really know what to say to me; you were stiff, aloof, unnatural. And just after you both went to bed, I guessed what the problem was. I'm not certain, obviously, but I'll be surprised if I'm wrong. After all, it's a few weeks since you were at the pub, either of you – it being a very heavy period on the farm and so forth. And since you were last there I would have been seen in there with somebody – and I would be willing to bet that you know who it is. Heather said you had chatted to that Mr Baldwin last night, and I see him as being the kind of man who thrives on spreading gossip and tittle tattle – would I be right?"

Her father nodded. "Phil Miller – far cry from an evening class." As soon as he had made the comment he had regretted it. Sarcasm, and implied resentment over his daughter deceiving

140

them as to her whereabouts on certain evenings, would not be constructive – though he was hurt that she had lied to them both.

"Yes, Phil Miller. And I'm sorry about the evening classes, Dad. Not that it's total deception; for I did start going to them in Tavistock back in April. The course was rather boring though, and the lecturer was hopeless, so after three weeks I stopped going to them. It seemed, however, a ready made excuse for me to go out evenings and have you or Heather babysit without further explanation. Still, it was wrong – and I am truly sorry."

Her father smiled. "Forget it, my love. It's not important. You and Phil Miller, though – that's different. That could be very important."

"No it's not – not at the moment, anyway. We are – as the tired phrase goes – just good friends. But he has been so kind and helpful to me since Simon's death, you know. You've probably seen him bringing in huge stocks of wood and coal for the fires back in the winter. And anything I needed from the village shop he would get for me. Naturally for his kindness and attention I would offer him cups of tea and coffee – and we'd chat. He's an intelligent man – with a marvellous sense of humour. And he – he has a certain charm about him. Not a sophisticated one, but an attractive one nonetheless."

"And he's good-looking," muttered her father, a gentle smile playing around his lips.

His daughter eyed him keenly, almost defiantly. "Extremely good-looking," she agreed, a rather sharp tone in her voice. She shrugged her shoulders. "Anyway, just a few weeks ago I was walking back from the village with Robert in the push-chair. It was a lovely evening back in May and I felt like a nice long walk and took the opportunity to post some letters in the box outside the Post Office. On the way back I walked past the pub and sitting at a table outside on his own was Phil. On seeing me he came over and insisted I join him for a drink. I could see no harm in it – and I really was thirsty by this time – so I joined him. All I had was a coke, and was with him for about an hour – and Robert slept throughout. But afterwards I realised that I enjoyed it. So when a few days later he asked me to meet him at the pub again, I agreed; and now I've probably been up there with him – what – half a dozen times perhaps. We've been nowhere else, mind you – just the pub."

"It wouldn't matter if you had, Alison," said her father in casual tones. "You're a widow, and he's a bachelor. Whatever either of you do, it's your business entirely."

"Oh yes – I know that," agreed his daughter – firmly. "And whilst I will always listen to your views Dad, and take note of what you say, the decisions which affect my life, my future – and that of Robert, of course – will be taken by me, and me alone. It's always been that way with me though, hasn't it?" she added confidently.

"Always," he agreed. "If you made up your mind to something, then the devil in hell wouldn't change it. Your mother will never be dead as long as you are alive, Alison."

His daughter smiled. "You've said that before, Dad." A slightly apprehensive expression crossed her face. "What do you think of Phil?" she asked, the tone of her voice suggesting that whilst she would go her own way in life, her father's opinion on the young man with whom she was friendly was one which was of some relevance to her.

"I only really know him as an employee," he replied. He shrugged his shoulders. "He always seems a decent enough fellow. He's hard working, reliable, good-natured – though he's got a hell of a temper on him. I was told this when he came to work for us, and on a couple of occasions I've seen him erupt. Mind you, knowing he's a touch volatile, Frank Morton has wound him up – but when he goes he explodes like a bomb. It doesn't last long, though – and there's certainly no malevolence with him, but it's wicked whilst it lasts. In fact, I would think he could become violent given the circumstances. But then, it's not a massive fault, is it?"

"No, not at all," agreed his daughter. "Most of us have our paddies, after all. And I know about his temper – he has warned me against it. And he says that his father has got a similar temper – which is why they find it so hard to work together."

"Oh yes – that is so. That's why he stopped working full-time at Holly Park and, eventually, came to work here – because he and his dad were falling out constantly; this forced his mother to lay down the law. She said that he could not work at home on the farm – except in a part-time way – until his father retired. He still lives at Holly Park, of course, and helps out on occasions, but he and his father's relationship has always been so volatile that poor

Mrs Miller found it impossible to tolerate their constant rows and bickering when working together. Yet, they think the world of each other. In fact, I was talking about Phil to Jack at Tavistock Market a couple of months ago, and he was on about what a fine chap he is and so forth. He certainly expects Phil to take over Holly Park when he and Sally retire – which could be sooner rather than later, Jack not being in the best of health or so I'm told."

"No he's not, Dad – heart trouble, according to Phil," interjected his daughter. "I think Phil worries about him a great deal – and about Holly Park. Although it's not a particularly large farm, there is still more than enough work there to keep a fit man extremely busy; Jack, of course, is not a fit man, so he's unable to do as much as he would like – and, indeed, which is necessary – so the place is going downhill rapidly according to Phil. He helps his father, of course, when he has got a bit of spare time – but has precious little of that, especially this time of the year. It worries him, the deterioration at the farm. He was born there, after all, and unlike Bray Barton, which we rent, it's a place his parents own. So he sees the value diminishing, which concerns him business-wise, along with the overall quality of the farm, which offends him professionally."

Her father nodded. "I'm sure you are right, my love. And I reckon the day is not that far away when Phil will give notice to us and go off and farm Holly Park – even though he and his dad will have a row every day. Mind you, if Jack's health is so bad he is unable to farm it himself, then he will just have to swallow his pride, sit back and let Phil get on with it."

George Tennant was to think of that early morning conversation with his daughter some six months later when on a bitter January morning Phil Miller gave a week's notice.

"It's Dad, Mr Tennant," said he to his employer – whom he had always addressed in such formal, courteous fashion. "He had another nasty turn, heart-wise, last week, and the doctor has told him he's got to retire – no ifs or buts about it. Stubborn as a mule mind you – refused point blank to do so. But Mum got at him, and when she really gets going, she's more than a match for Dad. Anyway, they are going to retire – officially and fully. And I'm going to take over. Technically it's going to happen at Easter, but I'll be running things there with immediate effect."

143

"Mum and Dad going to carry on living in the farmhouse, Phil?"

"No – they'll be retiring to a bungalow on the edge of the village. It works out just right for them really. The bungalow belonged to my gran and grandad on mother's side. Well, Grandad Coleman died several years back and Gran about five years ago. Mother's an only child, so the bungalow was left to her. Well, being mother – got more sense and foresight than both me and Dad put together, she has – she decided not to sell the place as Dad wanted her to but to rent it out on short term tenancies so that it would be available for them if or when they wanted to retire. Well, as luck would have it, the last tenants left at Christmas so it's empty now. Mum had planned to let it again at Easter, but when Dad had his attack last week she called the estate agents to tell them that it would not be let again; she then told Dad what was going to happen."

"So, she retired him, Phil, eh?" George Tennant asked the question with a broad smile playing about his lips; whilst he did not know Sally Miller well, what he did know of her suggested she was a pleasant, but somewhat formidable lady who would not hesitate to take a major decision affecting the lives of her family and the future of the farm – and would expect to have that decision adhered to.

"In effect, yes," her son agreed. "Anyway, they will be moving out in a few weeks, and I'll be left the house to live in and the farm to run."

"All on your own?"

"At the moment, yes." The question posed and the answer given were both simple and apparently straightforward, but both knew there was a certain innuendo involved. For since her conversation with her father the previous summer concerning her friendship with Phil, Alison had, during the autumn and winter period, spent an ever-increasing amount of time with the young man. They had long since moved beyond just the occasional visit to the local pub. The cinema in Plymouth, plus dancing there as well, visits to the Wharf at Tavistock for live theatre, which Alison greatly enjoyed, visits to the races at Newton Abbot, sometimes dinner at a decent local restaurant or hotel – Phil had taken his employer's attractive daughter to such venues increasingly over the months. He had even taken her, just a couple of

Saturdays earlier, to see his beloved Plymouth Argyle play and Alison, though not really a football fan, had enjoyed the afternoon immensely, finding the atmosphere created by a largish crowd most exhilarating.

Because of this, George saw Phil's statement that he was moving into Holly Park farmhouse on his own – at present – as being a broad hint that sooner rather than later he anticipated sharing it with somebody else. And it was less than two months after Easter – a bright, breezy day in early June – that he learnt Mr Miller was to be joined in the house by a wife and a stepson.

The news was brought to him originally – and inadvertently – by young Ben Small, a seventeen-year-old lad whose build was the exact opposite of his name, and who was the latest recruit to the staff at Bray Barton. For realising that with poor Simon gone, and Phil leaving, the farm would be gravely under-staffed – especially with summer coming on – Heather pointed out to her husband that they needed to take somebody on urgently. However, with Bray Barton's income being eroded by escalating overheads eating away at static returns, she suggested they avoided paying a full man's wage in the short term by employing a keen youngster, eager to learn. And it proved surprisingly easy to find one. For just a couple of days after the decision was taken to employ a teenager at Bray Barton, the ideal candidate evolved over a pint of bitter in the Peter Tavy Inn.

George had dropped in for a drink on a warm evening after collecting a dozen ewes which had wandered off and been corralled in the high walled carpark next to the village hall. With the help of folk living in the neighbouring cottages, the errant sheep had been driven up into the high domed horse-box which was to be their transport, and the high tailgate closed behind them. Feeling a touch thirsty and aware there was nothing spoiling at Bray Barton, he had stopped the tractor and box outside the pub and gone in for the cure to his thirst. Once there, he had fallen into conversation with Adam Small, who lived almost next door to the hostelry and who was shepherd up at Langford Ridge, a bleak farm about a mile north of Bray Barton. And amongst other news, the shepherd was spreading the information that his son Ben, who was seventeen and had always wanted to be a soldier, had become one some three months earlier but surprisingly not taken to the life – or the discipline anyway –

g

and had left the service of Her Majesty the previous day. "Silly young devil," his father grunted. "Set up for life he was, in the forces. God knows what he'll do now."

"What does he want to do?" asked George.

"Well, I fancy he wouldn't mind working on the land – anyway, for the time," opined his father. "Till he's sorted himself out and made up his mind as to what he wants to do in the future. Though I wouldn't be surprised if he didn't do farm work for the rest of his days. Always enjoyed helping me up at Langford Ridge, he has – and Farmer Bowman thinks the world of him. Trouble is, though, that he's got a boy of his own, as you know – Gordon – so there's no labour wanted up there. Hopefully something'll come along fairly soon; me and the missus can't keep him for very long – and we shouldn't have to, come to that."

"Well, Adam," replied George instantly, "something has already come along. I want Ben to work at Bray Barton."

So it was that the young fellow came to work for Heather and George – and had not been at the farm more than a couple of weeks when he unwittingly gave his employers information not previously known to them, but which came as no major surprise.

He had come into the kitchen one morning to receive his work instructions for the day and had commented to Heather when about to leave, "Lovely big house this, Mrs Tennant, isn't it? And it'll soon seem even bigger with just you and the boss – and the little maid, of course – in it, won't it?"

George had been a touch taken aback by this, and had asked Ben what his comments meant.

The lad had looked puzzled, then replied, "Well, when your daughter marries Phil Miller, boss. July or August, isn't it? That's what everybody is saying up the pub, anyway."

There was a general air of bemusement within the large kitchen at that moment – the lad being so because he failed to realise the originality of what he was saying as far as his employers were concerned, and Heather and George likewise owing to the unexpected news which had just come their way, from such an indirect source.

When Ben left the house to go about his work, George made an instant decision. "It seems to me, Heather, that whilst Alison has the right to do what she wants, she does have some sort of moral obligation to tell us – certainly courtesy would dictate as

146

much at any rate."

"It could all be tittle tattle," replied his wife, softly, anxious to pour some balm on her husband's annoyance and hurt. "You know what the village is like. Perhaps they are just putting two and two together – what with Phil now moved into the farm on his own, and going out with Alison quite regularly – and making, well, five," she concluded, rather lamely.

"Or four," he rasped. "I fancy it's four Heather, don't you? I've an idea they are going to get married. And I don't mind that; not that it's my place to mind it, come to that. Alison has got her own life to lead and she must lead it. And I fancy Phil will make her a decent enough husband – and young Robert an adequate father, which is so very important. He's a good enough fellow on the whole – hard working, responsible and, from what I can gather, he would appear to think the world of Alison – and Robert too, for that matter. I don't like his temper, mind you. It's not often it erupts but I've seen him in a paddy a couple of times and he is like a man demented. Still, we've all got our faults. It's just that if she has agreed to marry him, I really do not know why she hasn't told us. After all, next to Robert, we are the closest relatives she has got; I mean, well, I mean – I'm her father for God's sake."

"Yes, you are. And you should be told about it – if it's true," replied Heather calmly. "It seems to me, George, that the best way to settle your mind, one way or another, is to go through to see Alison now and ask her – this very minute. Then you will know – we all will; and we shall know where we all stand."

Seeing, as he usually did, the wisdom of his wife's words, George Tennant promptly went to see his daughter to ascertain whether or not the large Bray Barton farmhouse would soon be inhabited by just his wife, his daughter and himself.

Alison was neither embarrassed nor offended at her father's blunt question concerning the rumours that she was about to marry Phil Miller and take herself off to be mistress of Holly Park.

"How these tales have got about Dad, I really do not know," she explained in her forthright, honest way. "A lot of it is pure gossip – though it is not without some foundation. For Phil has asked me to marry him – though that was only last week. And I have said nothing to you or Heather because I have said nothing

147

to him; he is still awaiting my answer."

"And when will you give it, do you think?"

"Probably within the next couple of days – on Saturday, I expect. I'm seeing him on Saturday evening, you see. I will almost certainly give him my answer then."

"I know it's none of my business, Alison – but have you made a decision? Obviously you can tell me to mind my own business," he added, defensively.

"It is your business, Dad – and Heather's. For if I marry Phil, then I move out of this house, which will obviously affect you both. And – yes, I have made a decision. And strangely enough, I came to it last night. I have taken my time over it because there is more than just me to consider, isn't there?"

"Robert."

"Exactly – it has got to be right for him every bit as much as it has got to be right for me." She stopped, smiled, then continued. "Phil's marvellous with him Dad, he really is. He will probably never be quite as good with him as Simon would have been – he is not his natural father and that shows at times. But I feel he really does love him – just as he loves me."

"So you are going to marry him, my dear?"

"Yes Dad – I am."

George Tennant looked at his daughter for several seconds, a serious expression upon his face. Then his look moved readily from concern to pleasure – and he kissed his daughter gently upon the cheek, a quite rare show of affection from him.

"Then I wish you much happiness, Alison – now and always."

Chapter Seventeen

Alison Jenkinson married Phil Miller in Peter Tavy Church on a blustery Saturday morning in early October, and for the second time in her life was given in marriage by her father. And for reasons he was never to fully comprehend, George was to remark long afterwards that he felt closer to his daughter at the moment when he 'gave her away' for the second time than he had done at any other time in his life.

And it was very much a family occasion with Heather as Companion of Honour, Nicola as a pretty and proud bridesmaid and little Robert as a none too enthusiastic page-boy. Martin and Sylvia had travelled down for the wedding along with their son Jimmy, a fine, strongly built lad now in his early teens. And they had pleased Heather and George by accepting their invitation that they spend a few days at Bray Barton. "We've plenty of room – and rooms," as Heather had accurately put it. The offer was accepted with alacrity, the Guildford based couple always enjoying the west Country pace, and way of life – if not the weather.

So it was a good day, Alison's wedding day, and there was a feeling in the air that whilst she and her new husband were very different in backgrounds and temperament, they possessed a deep mutual love, and a very real desire to merge their disparate lives.

The day following the wedding was not nearly so good though, for it brought an incident which concentrated George's mind regarding whether or not he should continue to drive. It happened midway through Sunday afternoon. Heather, Nicola and he had been taken out to lunch at a hotel the other side of Tavistock by Martin and Sylvia and on his return he had changed into working gear, and was in the process of taking half a dozen bales of hay to some fine steers up in the Well Field. He had opened the gate to the field leading from the rutted lane, driven the tractor and 'linkbox' into the field, then got off again to close the gate behind him. He got back onto the tractor, put it into first gear, released the hand brake – then everything went black before his eyes. How long he was unconscious he did not really know, but he came around to find himself slumped over the tractor steering wheel, with the old machine chugging slowly, but inexorably, on its way relentlessly. Fortunately in lying across the wheel, he had turned it slightly to the right so that it was following a wide, circuitous route – one which, if maintained, would avoid permanently all the dry stone walls which bounded the large enclosure. How many times he had gone around he knew not, but the indentation of the tractor tyres in the spongy turf showed it had been quite a number.

He knocked the tractor out of gear, applied the hand brake, and sat bolt upright in his seat, his hands clasped to his head. He was well aware of just how lucky he had been; what, for instance, if he had been driving a car on the highway. He shook his head as would a dog when dripping with water; it did not bear thinking about – so he simply would not do so. The fact was he had not been driving on the road, and he had not been at the wheel of a car. He had simply lost consciousness – for no more than a brief time, surely – at the wheel of an ancient, slow moving tractor in a lonely field where he could have done harm to nobody except himself. Certainly he would never have mown down any steers – they were far too swift of foot for that. And it was a fair bet the attack was nothing to do with his epilepsy. Rather it was probably alcohol induced. He had imbibed a goodly amount at the wedding the previous day, plus a few glasses of wine over the excellent lunch they had just enjoyed, Martin doing the driving. Also it had been a somewhat stressful, if exciting time, and he was getting rapidly to – in truth, had arrived at – the age when such things did his health no good.

So there appeared to him to be no reason why he should make a fuss – no reason to tell Heather about it and most definitely absolutely no point in informing the doctor. He would just ensure he drank a little less in future. With this decision made, he dismissed the matter, as best he could, from his mind.

The winter which followed Alison's marriage was a bitter one, a stiletto like north-east wind setting in just prior to the New Year and lasting, in greater or lesser degree, for the best part of six weeks. George remarked to his wife – virtually every day – that he could never recall being as cold in his entire life, only to be informed by Heather, with genial contempt, that such weather was anything but rare on or around Dartmoor. The wind, naturally, brought frost and snow, and added immensely to the winter feeding work at Bray Barton. Also, it meant that a great deal more forage than normal was consumed by the voracious beasts and that occasioned the necessity for George to buy some in – an unforeseen, and expensive situation. It was the first time since he had been at Bray Barton that there had been a necessity to put money into the pockets of the forage merchants, but Heather made him feel a little less culpable by saying that her father, in a hard winter, had occasionally needed to top up his fodder stores by buying in the odd lorry load. Not that the present situation was entirely unexpected. For the previous summer's harvest had been below average due to poorish weather, and Heather had commented then that they could be in trouble if there was a hard winter.

The heavy expenditure on the extra forage could not have come at a worse time, for the Tennants, early in the winter, had passed over a large cheque to Alison to buy out her share of Bray Barton. They had expected the new Mrs Miller to broach the subject of Heather and George purchasing the twenty-four per cent she held in the tenancy of the farm at some time, but were a little taken aback that she voiced it as early as she did. The reason, though, was logical and straightforward – Holly Park was under-capitalised. For while Phil's parents had made the farm over to him lock, stock and barrel – a truly generous gesture to their only child – they had, naturally, retained for themselves, to eke out their old age, the meagre profits they had made over the years. So the newly married couple needed working capital and whilst they could probably have borrowed from the bank, it was far more sensible of them to sell Alison's interest in Bray Barton.

Heather and George could have refused to buy her share, of course – for a time, at least – saying, truthfully, that to purchase it they could well over-extend themselves at the bank, neither of them inclined to touch their tolerably substantial capital put by for retirement or unforeseen circumstances. With Alison being family, however, and she and her new husband's need being greater than theirs, it was never a serious option. So a sum was agreed with, and paid to, the Millers, and with the worryingly high winter expenditure on forage and so forth, the overdraft was allowed to bloat. The Tennant's bank manager at the Midland in Tavistock began to get just a little concerned over its exceptional size, but before he actually galvanised himself to take any action, June had arrived following an unusually warm – and wet – May, and a promising bunch of Bray Barton store cattle had flourished sufficiently for them to be sold at Tavistock Market, a sizeable cheque thus being paid into the farm's current account, staying the bank manager's hand in terms of his writing a cautionary letter to the tenants of Bray Barton.

And even better was to come, for although the winter had been hard, the lamb crop had been above average, and the lush spring and early summer grass had brought on the young sheep faster than normal; thus, a far higher than usual number of lambs were sent to market during July and August – when prices were relatively high – ensuring that financially Bray Barton enjoyed a good spell. Also, a heavy hay and silage harvest meant that no matter how severe the winter which followed, there should be ample forage for the hungry stock.

A mildish, though inevitably damp autumn followed, with plenty of late keep for the stock, this to be followed by a crisp, frosty, but not unpleasant early winter. So as George and Heather sat down to their Christmas dinner in Bray Barton's large dining-room with their daughter Nicola, they could look back upon quite a good year in terms of their business.

Unfortunately, for their guests Alison and Philip – accompanied by young Robert, now a fine lad almost of school age – the year had not been as kind. For a succession of disasters had ravaged their none too great financial resources – even though augmented by the cheque from the Tennants for Alison's share of Bray Barton. Three prime milking cows had died – all through misfortune rather than any lack of expertise on the part of the farmer – and many thousands of pounds had been spent on machinery, either patching up the old or, in the case of a tractor and various implements, buying new. For Jack Miller had been the very worst of farmers when it came to machinery – failing to replace that which was nearing the end of its mechanical life and oblivious to the need to give even the sparsest attention to that

152

which was still basically sound.

Thus did his son and daughter-in-law have to pick up the tab – and it did nothing to help the viability of Holly Park. This, though, was not the only problem. Farming, ever a capricious occupation to even the most experienced and shrewd countryman, could be a malicious, almost heart-breaking way of making a living when in the hands of a young man without experience of making decisions. And this was an exact description of Phil Miller. He knew his craft well enough, but during the erratic, stormy times he had spent at Holly Park with his father, Jack, naturally enough, had made the decisions on the farm, whilst his mother had made them indoors. And at Bray Barton, of course, he had employers to decide matters. And unfortunately the difficulty in making decisions at all on the one hand, or making them far too hastily on the other, were compounded by his volatile nature. And he most assuredly had that – as Alison soon found out.

Essentially an easy going, pleasant young man, he was nonetheless – as was, of course, well known in the community – subject to enormous mood swings, and a truly dangerous temper. And whilst such aberrations of his natural personality were not regular occurrences, they were sufficiently common to alarm his wife, especially when he had been drinking. Not that he could have been described as having a serious drink problem, but there were times – too many of them, in truth – when he came back from the Peter Tavy Inn much the worse for wear, having driven home. It was a habit of which Alison strongly disapproved on three accounts; that it had an undesirable affect on his personality, it made him extremely vulnerable in terms of losing his driving licence – "and where would we be then, Phil?" as she would comment perceptively – and squandered money they could ill afford. Indeed, she became increasingly angry that her earnings as a part-time teacher were used as much to subsidise his drinking habit as they were for more positive and constructive aspects of their life and that of her son – and his stepson.

Despite this and his often aggressive attitude towards both she and Robert – though he had never been violent even in the slightest way – he was essentially a kind and thoughtful man and his wife had no doubts of his love for her. Thus their marriage, though not without its squalls, was sound enough – though it would have been given greater security in every way if Phil was more of a master of his profession, the planning ahead, and general running of all aspects of a hill farm.

This lack of accomplishment on the young farmer's part was in no way helped with the sudden death of his father, Jack, fewer than six months after that Christmas Day which Alison and he had spent at Bray Barton. Jack Miller's heart had long been an organ of extreme fragility and it came as no real surprise – though it was still very much a shock to his wife and son – when one sunny morning he keeled over whilst mowing the back lawn of his bungalow. That he was dead before hitting the ground was some small comfort to his widow – or so the doctor had suggested – but having always been a very close couple she grieved greatly. And she felt angry that, "A good man like Jack, a friend to all who knew him, had been taken at sixty, whilst the world is full of folk who'll do nobody a good turn, and they seem to live forever," as she put it.

Sally Miller, however, was quite a resilient woman and within twelve months had come to terms with her husband's death, forging a new life for herself – to a certain extent. She spent quite a bit of time at Holly Park helping out – a crucial contribution with Alison continuing to provide vital augmentation to the family budget through her teaching – and also, when a vacancy came about at the local parish council, put her name forward, fought a by-election, and won it. Born, bred and having always lived locally, she had ever taken a keen and, at times, an aggressive interest in village matters and had often opined to Jack that she would not have minded becoming a councillor one day. Active farming was too time-consuming for her to even think about public life, but now retired, and with the vacuum of widowhood crying out for something new to fill it, at least partially, now was surely the right time to go into local government; so she did.

If the twelve months following Jack Miller's death marked a period of adjustment to a new way of life for his widow, for George and Heather Tennant it was a year during which two major happenings brought them great benefits and peace of mind. The first came during a visit from Martin, Sylvia and grandson Jimmy. They came to spend Christmas at Bray Barton, and made what would have been a most enjoyable time normally, a truly

154

memorable one. For on Christmas Day, after the presents — cascading invitingly about the tree – had been opened, Martin produced an envelope from his pocket and gave it to his father. "An extra present, Dad – for you and Heather," he said, a broad smile on his lips. "Though perhaps present is not the right word. Rather it's the partial repayment of a debt, one that has caused both Sylvia and me more heartache than you might realise."

George gave his son a somewhat uncomprehending look, then promptly opened the envelope – and slid a cheque from its depths. "A cheque – for one hundred and twenty thousand pounds?" The words came out in the form of a gasp, whilst the expression on his face registered total bemusement.

"That's right, Dad – a goodly part of the amount we owe you and Heather. It was one hundred and forty thousand pounds that you had to pay up a few years back to honour the guarantee you had given the bank on our behalf; and just after your marriage as I recall. A dreadful time to beg money, and I – no, we – have felt nothing but guilt about it ever since. Well, we can now start feeling a little less guilty, whilst you have a cheque to put in the bank which I'm sure will be of use. Farming is one of the more precarious of professions these days, I am reliably told. Mind you, we still owe you a few thousand yet, obviously. Another twenty – plus interest, naturally. We cannot quite afford that at present, but it will not be forgotten, you can be sure of that."

With George standing as still as a statue, gazing unblinkingly at the cheque which he held in his hand, obviously totally overwhelmed by this so unexpected mega boost to their fortunes, it was left to his wife to articulate their thanks.

"This is wonderful, Martin – Sylvia," she cried out in pure joy. "I won't say the bailiffs are at the door – or anywhere near it – but times are not easy on the land what with BSE, low returns and one thing and another, as you rightly say. And not owning Bray Barton, we do not have the security to ever be able to expect too much leeway at the bank. So this cheque will be a Godsend; it will give us security for years to come no matter what might happen. Thank you – oh, thank you so much." Promptly she embraced them both, then swept emergent tears from her eyes with the deftest flick of her right hand.

"No need to thank us," replied Sylvia – a touch embarrassed by this emotive show of gratitude. "We are merely repaying a debt –

and we've still not paid it in full."

"But where did you get such money from?" cried the farmer's wife — immediately regretting her question. "Ignore that, please. I'm sorry; it's none of my business where the money came from."

Martin laughed. "There's no secret about it, Heather — we've not robbed a bank or suchlike. No — it's Sylvia's inheritance."

"As you may remember, my mother died about eighteen months ago," said his wife, taking up the story. "Well, it's taken until nearly now to wind up her estate — and sell her house. But the cheque is the result of that; I'm an only child, of course, and the sole beneficiary. So when the final cheque came to me a few weeks back — after the lawyers and tax people had had their large share, of course — I suggested that we should put a bit of it by for Jimmy, and the rest of it we give to you, with our thanks and with the assurance that we will, as we said just now, pay back the rest in the not too distant future."

"But what of yourselves?" asked George Tennant, his voice so emotional it was little more than a croak. "I mean, you lost virtually everything a few years back; this would have put you on your feet again."

"We are already on them, Dad," Martin replied. "I've a good job, as you know, whilst Sylvia works part-time which brings in enough to pay the mortgage. So we are doing quite well on the whole and whilst a cheque of that size would have fitted nicely into our bank balance, it's only right you should have the bulk of it. We will never forget what you did — and we shall see that the rest is paid to you in due course."

So it was that the Tennants became 'comfortable' financially, both of them happy to let the money gain some interest until the time came — and it probably would come — when it was needed.

If Christmas brought them a massive financial boost, then a phone call just a couple of weeks after Easter brought them a bonus of a very different kind. For the call came from Canada — from Derek — and lasted for more than an hour, causing George to comment later that he was glad he would not have to pay for it. But the call was as important a one as ever could come over the wires to Bray Barton, for it established, to a considerable extent, the direction in which the farming, and future ownership of the place would develop.

The basic upshot of the call was that Derek and Elaine

156

expressed a desire to return to Britain, to Peter Tavy and to Bray Barton — permanently. They had enjoyed their years in Canada; also, they had prospered, reasonably. But the time had come to make a decision long term — forced on them. For cousin Danny was looking for a financial boost and had broached the subject of Elaine and Derek buying into the farm as had been mooted at the very beginning. So it was crossroads time, and the couple were well aware of it.

They could sell their cottage in Peter Tavy, and possibly their twenty-five per cent stake in Bray Barton as well, put that money into Danny's farm, and pursue a Canadian way of life for probably the rest of their days — or they could put everything down to experience, tell Danny they had enjoyed their Canadian sojourn, and return home.

Surprisingly, despite the fact they had enjoyed life in the new world, and the lifestyle, neither had truly settled to it; they had found life full, but not fulfilling, interesting but not really satisfying. Thus, they had both, independently, come to the conclusion that when a decision had to be made as to their long-term future — and they knew ultimately it would have to be made — they would turn their eyes eastwards and return from whence they had come.

September was the month they planned to return — it would give them plenty of time to tie up the loose ends in Canada and, also, the short term lease they had granted the young couple who had rented their cottage since they had gone abroad conveniently ran out at the end of August. As to the work Derek would do to earn his living, Bray Barton could offer him plenty. Indeed, George and Heather hoped, when hearing of the Maunders' return from Canada, that it would be early summer rather than late, for with Phil working his own acres there was a serious shortage of staff at Bray Barton, George and Frank Morton, along with the enthusiastic but very inexperienced teenager, Ben Small, being the only full-time workers on the place — though Heather was once again making a major contribution. Also, there were a couple of fellows from Peter Tavy, technically drawing the dole, who were happy to augment their meagre benefit with some healthy though hard work on the farm.

However, George found it a little easier to face the seemingly non-stop work, that was life at Bray Barton that summer, contemplating the approaching help which Derek would provide – along with considerable expertise. And that extra pair of hands, and the professionalism innate within a man born and bred to the land, would almost certainly ensure that future summers would be just a little less hectic.

Chapter Eighteen

Both Heather and George looked forward with enormous enthusiasm to the return of Derek, Elaine and Louise – the promised day being the last Thursday in September. Yet it was destined to be a day which was marred. Not by anything concerning Derek and family, though, who were due to arrive at Plymouth railway station – from Heathrow – late that afternoon, but rather due to the fraught problems of another member of the family. For about eleven o'clock that morning, a car screeched to a halt in the yard at Bray Barton, and a woman ran from it towards the back door of the house.

George was coming from the paddock beyond the yard and recognised the car as being Alison's red Ford Escort, and the woman running to, and entering, the house as being his daughter. What ailed her he knew not, but it had to be something major to cause her, of all people – nearly always seemingly in strict control of her emotions and actions – to act in such an alarming way.

All thoughts of the routine tasks he was performing sped from his mind as he himself ran towards the house – there was something amiss with his daughter and she obviously needed help. He reached the back door quite quickly, thrust it open and was in the kitchen within seconds, where he was confronted with a sobbing daughter who was being comforted by Heather, whose arms enveloped her in a protective embrace.

Alison swung around on hearing the closing of the kitchen door – and George was shocked at what he saw. For her face was red and blotchy with crying but, more ominously, there was a livid mark emblazoned on her left cheek – obviously imprinted there by a blow.

"What is it, Alison – what's happened?" came her father's

159

frantic question. He went to her, and enveloped her in his arms, Heather releasing her as he did so. "What's happened, my love – tell me." His words now were softer – more controlled.

"It's Phil, Dad – he's – he's – he's on the verge of a breakdown, I'm sure he is."

"Did he cause that bruising on your cheek?"

She nodded. "It's the first time he has ever struck me . . ."

"And it'll be the last," rasped her father. "No daughter of mine is going to be knocked about by anybody – and I'm going over to Holly Park to tell him, and in no uncertain manner."

"No, Dad – please no. As I say, he has never done it before – and as soon as it happened he regretted it, I could see that in his face. And I'm sure he would have apologised if I had given him a chance. The trouble was, I was so shocked I just ran out, jumped into the car, and rushed over here. I wish now I hadn't. It was an over-reaction – foolish and childish of me. Perhaps I should go home right away and talk it out with him." She started to move towards the door only to be stopped by her father.

"No, Alison – I don't want you going back there. If he's done it once, he'll do it again. Stay here with us – for a while, at least."

"I cannot stay here Dad – there's Robert apart from anything else. Anyway, I don't want to stay here. Holly Park's my home – Phil's my husband. My life is there – with both of them. I'm sorry to have behaved so stupidly; I'll be away home – right now."

With that, she rushed from the kitchen, half ran to the car and was, within seconds, well on the way back to Holly Park, leaving a bemused couple staring at each other in the kitchen.

"I think," said Heather slowly, and softly, "that we both need a cup of tea." And she promptly went to the sideboard to switch on the kettle, her husband slumping down onto the nearest chair.

He held his head in his hands for a few seconds, then looked at his wife as she poured boiling water into the teapot. "Well, Heather – what do you make of that. What's going on for heaven's sake? And what can we do?"

"To answer the last question first, not a lot," she replied as she walked to the table carrying a tray which bore teapot, beakers and milk. "We can only really help her if she wants us to, George – and as yet, I don't think she does."

"Then why did she rush all the way over here?"

"I think it was a reaction – she would, at present, no doubt consider it an over-reaction – to something which had shocked her temporarily. He hit her, George – the first time he had ever done so; quite probably the first time any man had ever done so. After all, I cannot imagine that Simon ever did, and I doubt very much you ever did even when she was a child; Simon was, and you are, too disciplined and gentlemanly to do anything like that. Phil Miller though, is a very different kettle of fish – all passion, emotion, anger – and joy – is Phil; up one minute, down the next; the temper of a devil, as we know, yet the heart of a lion at times, and the ability to be as kind, gentle and generous and affable as anybody I've ever met; and also to be witty and frank, the life and soul of any party. He's a creature of mood, George – he always has been and undoubtedly always will be. At present, I've a feeling his mood swings will be down more often than up; he is drinking a bit more than he should – Alison has told us that, and even if she hadn't, then half the parish would not hesitate to tell us – and, of course, he is worried. He's no businessman as we all know and in these days when margins are tight, a farmer needs to be as much businessman as stockman, to have as much knowledge of a balance sheet as of a baler. Phil has not got such abilities; also, despite his willingness to work all the hours sent, he is no great farmer; we have said often, haven't we, that despite the fact he was born and bred to it, he lacks judgement on so many farming matters and has a surprising lack of 'feel' for the land. Even though you have been at it a comparatively short time, you've infinitely more awareness and understanding of farming than he has – as an overall concept and way of making a living."

George said nothing, but was greatly touched – indeed, flattered – by his wife's compliment regarding his farming ability. For though Heather was ever quick to praise and was invariably generous with compliments, she was nonetheless a very truthful woman, and such kind words from her had to be earned. Her husband knew that the generous comment she had just put his way was sincere – totally. They did nothing, though, to lessen his worries concerning his daughter, and her marriage to a young man who was, increasingly, showing an attitude and character, which mitigated against respect.

Alison's marital problems, however, did slowly ease themselves to the back of his mind over the next few weeks, there being no further incidents at Holly Park, of which he was aware,

161

thus allowing the return and settling in of Derek, Elaine and Louise to take centre stage. And the trio had returned noticeably different people from those who had left four years earlier. In Louise's case, naturally, the principal change was a physical one – she had grown considerably.

Derek and Elaine had returned as a couple with a very different attitude to life. For it was almost instantly apparent, certainly in Derek's case, that his diffidence – and lack of confidence – was very much a thing of the past. A callow young man had left England's shores and a mature man of the world had returned. And something similar could be said of Elaine. For whilst she had always possessed more confidence than her husband, her travelling to the New World had given her self-possession and a measure of sophistication previously lacking. There could be no doubt that the time they had spent in Canada had been the making of Derek and Elaine Maunder.

This new found confidence of Derek's was rapidly to be seen in his work at Bray Barton. For he approached his tasks – many being of a type he had not done since he had left England – with enthusiasm, expertise and self-assurance. Also, whereas before he had always been a follower, now he was a leader. Not only did he get back into the routine of Devonshire hill farming very quickly, right from the start he made it plain to Heather and George, in both action and word, that he wanted a major say in everything concerning the farm – even though technically he only owned a quarter share – and really wished to make decisions, and put into practice some of the new ideas which had come his way in Canada.

In principle, his sister and brother-in-law welcomed this. George especially was pleased. Indeed, he was both relieved and delighted that there was now a man about seeing to the everyday running of the farm and willing to make decisions with vastly more knowledge of the job than himself. Frank Morton had long been of great help to him, of course, with his life-long knowledge of both farming and Dartmoor, but he was only an employee – decisions had fallen to George, though Heather's wise counsel had ever been vital in this direction. Now, though, Derek was there to take so much of that unwanted burden from his shoulders – and make life so very much more relaxing and comfortable for both Heather and himself.

By Christmas, the Maunders had settled back into Devonshire life and were planning for their long-term future. Part of these plans included their desire to buy a further twenty-five per cent of the tenancy of Bray Barton – from Heather and George of course, who owned seventy-five per cent of the total – and largely to fund the purchase by selling their cottage in Peter Tavy. Their home sold, they would then move into Bray Barton farmhouse and live there in the half previously occupied by Alison and Simon.

The proposals were put to Heather and George at Bray Barton on Boxing Day when Heather had the Maunder family over for lunch. They promised to give the ideas urgent consideration knowing full well they would agree to them – indeed, welcome them. For the house was far too big for just themselves and Nicola; whilst both justice and pragmatism suggested that Derek and Elaine should have an equal share in the farm – they would then have equal say and equal responsibility. Also, of course, a nice cheque would be lodged into the Tennant's bank account – along with Martin's major replacement – to give them very real security for a long time to come.

Thus it was before the New Year Heather told Derek that his proposals were totally acceptable to both herself and her husband, news which made the returned couple exceedingly happy.

Further news which was to please the couple was given by Elaine – that she was pregnant. A brother for Louise was most earnestly hoped for.

Alison and a rather taciturn Phil were also visitors to Bray Barton on Boxing Day. Neither had a great deal to say, though Alison appeared to be in reasonable humour. George, still angry with his son-in-law over his striking of his daughter, treated the young man coldly, though with basic courtesy, and was able to have some conversation with Alison. She assured him that Phil had not struck her since that morning three months previously, but that his moods were still erratic whilst the financial problems which bedevilled them showed no signs of disappearing.

"Phil sold some stock last month which will keep the wolves at bay for a few weeks, Dad," said his daughter, wearily, "but they'll be at the door again before long, of that there can be no doubt. What we shall do then, I really do not know. There's a limit to how much we can sell. I suppose the bottom of this downward spiral we appear to be in is the selling of Holly Park. That would pay off our debts, of course – but we would have little money left after that, and we would have no home. It doesn't bear thinking about." Tears at this point began to seep from her eyes and roll slowly down her cheeks.

Her father put his arms about her, kissed her gently on the cheek and made the sole pledge he possibly could – and one which, he knew, Heather would fully agree with even though he made it without consulting her; "We'll make sure that doesn't happen, Alison. If it ever gets to that stage – or even approaches it – then Heather and I will come up with financial guarantees, and even cash if necessary. In fact, we will do it now if it'll help in any way."

The words cheered his daughter. Her tears ceased, and a smile creased her face. "Thanks, Dad," she said, softly. "I do appreciate what you've said – and Phil will, as well. As to a loan now, I think perhaps we will hang on a little longer to see how things go. But it's wonderful to know you are there – like a safety net."

George Tennant would wonder for the rest of his life if that was the moment when his daughter's fate was settled. If only she had accepted his offer of cash there and then; if only the immediate problem and pressure of debt had been lifted from her – and, more importantly – her husband's shoulders.

But what was to happen might well have transpired even if a cheque had been made over to the couple – or so Heather opined, honestly and probably accurately.

It was less than four months later that the event which was to destroy, distort or simply change so many lives exploded, bringing police and tragic news to the door at Bray Barton early one fresh, sunny April morning just a few days after Easter. George had just left Derek and Frank Morton in the shippen where they were busy milking the herd, and returned across the yard to the kitchen for a cup of tea as was his habit.

No sooner had he entered the large warm room, and sat down at the table – to be handed a beaker of tea from Heather, who had only just arisen – than he heard the sound of a car engine outside. The couple glanced at each other, both aware that the clock was barely on half past seven, extremely early for a caller. Curious, George got up from the table, went to the window and looked out – and a disturbing sight greeted him.

"It's a police car," said he – his voice somewhat tense with

164

foreboding; police cars usually meant problems at any time of day if they called – at such a time as this, even the most law abiding of citizens would anticipate dire happenings.

He moved from the window to the door, opened it and observed a police inspector and WPC approaching. The inspector came up to the farmer framed in the doorway, touched the peak of his cap and enquired in soft, gentle tones, "Mr Tennant? Mr George Tennant?"

"Yes, that's me. What can I do for you?" The question was asked automatically – the answer, he knew, would bring pain.

"I'm Inspector Dawson from Tavistock Police Station – this is WPC Harvey," he indicated his female companion with a brief wave of his hand, and it was at that moment the farmer remembered an observation of a friend of his years back in London – 'If the police bring you bad news, they always bring a woman with them.'

"May we come in, sir?"

"Of course," muttered George. He stood aside to allow his visitors to pass by into the kitchen, where they were confronted by Heather, apprehension etched upon her features; she had, also, an awareness of the presence of the policewoman.

"This is my wife, Heather," said the farmer, softly.

The Inspector looked somewhat perplexed. "Good morning, Mrs Tennant," he said after a brief pause. "I am here concerning Mrs Alison Miller. You, Mr Tennant," he stated, with the tone of a man not at ease with uncertainty, "are Mrs Miller's father I believe?"

The farmer nodded.

"And Mrs Tennant is her – her . . ."

"Her stepmother," interjected the farmer, aware of the policeman's embarrassed confusion over the discrepancy in age between George and his wife, and the obvious impossibility of Heather being Alison's mother.

"Yes – yes, of course." The Inspector nodded his head in almost exaggerated fashion, relieved that the relationship had been established.

"Can we offer you some tea or coffee?" enquired Heather with her customary courtesy.

"No, Mrs Tennant, thank you." The Inspector glanced at her, then looked at her husband. "We have come concerning your daughter, Mr Tennant – as I said just now; I'm afraid, sir, you – and Mrs Tennant, of course – must prepare yourself for some very bad news. The fact is that your daughter is dead. Her husband called the police early this morning saying that he thought his wife was dead. We attended and found this sadly to be the case."

Heather Tennant rushed to her husband standing immobile in the middle of the kitchen, an expression of incomprehension upon his face. She put her arms around him and led him over to an easy chair standing before the big Aga cooker on the far side of the big room. Seeing him seated, she then turned and looked at the Inspector. "How did she die," she asked simply.

"I'm afraid she died violently, Mrs Tennant," said he softly, though briskly. "She was bludgeoned to death by the butt of a shotgun."

"Oh, my God, my God," stuttered Heather Tennant, whilst her husband gazed steadily ahead, both his mind and body paralysed with shock.

The Inspector gazed firstly at George Tennant, then at his wife. For a few seconds he appeared uncertain how to continue, but finally mouthed the words of nightmare. "We have made an arrest," he said, his tones now controlled. "Her husband, Philip Miller, has been charged with her murder."

Chapter Nineteen

That George Tennant came through the most agonising and traumatic period of his life with his reason intact, was down to Heather. Always a woman seemingly able to reach down deep into herself and draw strength, courage and fortitude from that inner well, she partially shielded her vulnerable husband – and step-grandson Robert, who with no mother now, had come to live with them – from as much of the pain as was possible during those dreadful months which elapsed between the doing of the deed and the trial. She was helped in this by the community. Heather had lived in that parish all of her life and her family had been there for generations. In an age when changing ways, priorities and standards had reached even rural Devon, she was seen as a rock of continuity and principle and local folk responded accordingly by giving George and herself all the moral and practical help they could.

The trial, at Plymouth Crown Court, was brief. Haggard looking, almost zombie-like Phil Miller, pleading guilty to the murder of his wife. His barrister had attempted to get his agreement that they intimate to the prosecution that the farmer would plead not guilty to murder but would accept manslaughter with the balance of the mind disturbed. Miller, though, would have none of that. His love for Alison had been very real, deep and intense, but through the eruption of that vile temper of his he had destroyed the lives of them both. In a statement to the court he told how he had come home in the early hours of that fateful morning much the worse for liquor, having drunk after hours at the pub, then consumed half a bottle of whisky whilst driving home in his battered car – a journey he could scarce remember.

He had drunk more than was good for him throughout most of

his adult life; during his early years, when single and not owning a farm, he had imbibed liquor simply because he liked it. Since his marriage, however, and his taking over of Holly Park, it had grown, steadily, more heavy and debilitating. A psychiatrist for the defence had stated in mitigation that Miller was an immature man who, whilst his love for his wife was central to his entire existence, was not gifted of any meaningful strength of character. Also, although capable of real hard work, there was a streak of indolent fecklessness about him, allied to a lack of commonsense and reality, especially in business and money matters, which would make him at best, a difficult, erratic man when stressed, at worst, a highly dangerous one. And with the farm he treasured sliding slowly, but inexorably from his grasp into that of the bank's and assorted creditors, he had exploded and destroyed a wife whom he loved as he had nobody else throughout his entire life.

His mother Sally, gave evidence in support of this. Resilient, courageous woman though she was, the violent death of her daughter-in-law, and the guilt of her only son combined to stretch her spirit almost to breaking point; yet drawing on every ounce of strength and character within her slight frame, she refused to allow that spirit to be rent asunder, and gave evidence of her son's outlook and nature – and weaknesses – in a calm, steady fashion. She told of his basic decency, his capacity to love, his generosity of spirit; she told also of his dark side, a vicious, almost maniacal temper which had been his bane ever since babyhood. He inherited his turbulent nature largely from his father; but in anger Phil had an uncontrollable malevolence, a capacity for harming others – mentally and physically – not possessed by his father. It was this vicious madness, his mother stated simply, brought to boiling point by the liquor, which had caused him to murder his wife and destroy his own life, in reality, all in a few seconds of mayhem. She said no more at the trial – and was destined to say little thereafter. For within two months of the trial which saw her son sentenced to life imprisonment, Sally Miller was dead.

She had lost her family either tragically, violently or judicially, in the space of but a couple of years, and she herself was destined to die in dreadful circumstances. For she was found one morning drowned in the turgid filth that was the slurry pit at Holly Park. Why she had visited the farm which had brought such tragedy to her life, and which had subsequently passed beyond both her ownership and her influence – the bank having repossessed it – no one knew, and none ever would know. It was assumed she had gone out there for reasons of nostalgia, had wandered around and had somehow fallen into a pit which had long since been in an abject state – and become highly dangerous. Thus, the coroner recorded a verdict of accidental death.

If she had drowned in a river, then the fact she was known to be very depressed would have brought notions of possible suicide. Nobody, however, including police and coroner, could believe that anyone would seek death by drowning in such a vile pit.

Her death was but another blow to the Tennants – "Is there no end?" as George enquired, plaintively of nobody in particular. And, "Is there any purpose to it all?" as he enquired of his wife at almost the same time, a question which brought a predictable response of fierce positivity from Heather.

"Of course there's a purpose, George – how can you doubt there is? Good God, man, few of us live life solely for ourselves and those who do rarely find fulfilment. We, though, live for others, like most folk. Hopefully we live also for each other – but we live as well for our daughter, our Nicola, and our grandson, Robert. There's our purpose in life, George, bringing them up – and it's a joint venture. A daughter needs a father every bit as much as she needs a mother; and Robert, poor little mite – if ever anybody needed love and security, then it is him; if ever anybody needed us it is him. His real father died tragically, and his mother was murdered by his stepfather. The scars which he must carry – even at his young age – are horrendous, George. He has nobody to give him a home and bring him up, and give him a decent life – and love – but us. There's your purpose, George – there's our purpose; don't ever forget it."

The words hit home, with George making a valiant, and reasonably successful effort to claw his way back towards a normal life. And that effort was given impetus, as always, by Heather – this time indirectly, he being warmed and motivated by the heat of her excitement one fine day in early spring. It was a Friday, nearing lunch-time, when George, walking across the yard from the tractor shed, deep in thought, had his reverie shattered by the honking of a car horn. He glanced behind him to

h

see Heather speeding across the yard from the gate leading from the road.

She drove much faster than normal to the back of the house, screeched to a halt and jumped from the car in a state obviously of great exhilaration. In her right hand she clutched some papers and waved them at her husband with all the enthusiasm of a steward brandishing the chequered flag in the general direction of the winner of a Grand Prix.

"George," she cried, espying her husband, "look at this – just look at this."

The farmer had rarely, if ever, seen his wife as high. Indeed, so shrill and loud was her voice, that she woke her baby nephew, Paul, Derek and Elaine's new son and part heir, who had been sleeping the slumber of the innocent in the farmhouse. The baby's cries, though, were not heard in the yard – Heather continued to make far too much noise for that.

"It's Holly Park, George – it's on the market. The bank own it now, of course, and are going to sell it to recoup their losses and pay off poor Alison's and Phil's debts. It's coming up for auction in a month – at Tavistock Guildhall." Heather's delight was excessive – and the reason for it was something of a mystery to George.

"It was inevitable the bank would sell it, Heather," replied he, almost off-handedly. "They have got to recoup their money somehow. But I don't see why you're so excited about it – it doesn't affect us in any direct way."

"But it does, George – that's the point. Oh, I'm not surprised you do not see it – you're not the best in the world when it comes to vision. And, to be honest, I must confess that the full possibilities only struck me this morning – hit me like a bolt of lightning. I was in Tavistock pannier market buying some salad stuff, when Jane Godfrey – you wouldn't know her, but I went to school with her; she lives down at Bere Alston now – said that she had seen in the *Tavistock Times* that Holly Park was up for auction. 'Lovely farm,' she said – and she knows it because she lived all her life in Peter Tavy prior to marrying – 'be an excellent buy for someone. And I expect it will go cheaply; farming is such these days that there's not any great demand for land anymore – and the recession has seen to it that there aren't the rich business people about to buy up the farmhouses there used to be, not locally

170

anyway!' She works part-time in an estate agents at Launceston these days, George, so she knows what she is talking about regarding values and suchlike. No sooner had she said it than I saw it all clearly and rushed around to the auctioneers to get the details – and here they are."

She brandished the papers once more. "George, we have to talk," she continued, breathlessly. "There's much to be gone into, I know, but I believe strongly in the hand of fate, as you well know. Holly Park was in our family, thanks to Alison, which is significant. It is about one hundred and fifty acres – an ideal size for this area – and has total moor and commoners' rights, like Bray Barton. With Paul's birth, Elaine and Derek have a son who might well keep the name going on Bray Barton for at least another generation – and that's important. Also, it will become no easier for two families to make a living out of a hill farm they do not own; plus, it has been the ambition of a lifetime to own my own farm – and I know you feel much the same way nowadays. And we've got Nicola's future to think about – and Robert, of course. Either, or both, could want to farm in the future – and I see no way that Bray Barton could accommodate them in that direction. In fact a drove of us attempting to eke a living from the place would bankrupt all of us. And George, thanks to Martin and Sylvia – and to Derek and Elaine buying back an equal share in our tenancy of Bray Barton – we have a considerable sum of money in the bank. Granted it's our nest-egg – our insurance against the deluge. But perhaps it could be put to positive use now; perhaps it could be used to buy our future – to ensure success, rather than be a bulwark against failure. George, I think it is more than likely we have sufficient capital, without borrowing a penny, to buy Holly Park and, hopefully, to fund the stocking of it, both live and dead. And if we did this, then we would leave Bray Barton to Derek and Elaine – though still keeping an interest for the time. Anyway, I don't suppose they could afford to buy us out fully at present. We would move into Holly Park, George – you, me, Nicola and Robert and we would, for the first time in our lives, farm land which we owned, every stick, stone and blade of grass. What do you think, George – how do you feel about it?"

Her husband had stood statuesque before the joyous torrent of words which had cascaded from his wife's lips, allowing them to

171

wash over him like a warm invigorating tidal wave. He was a little numb, though there was within himself, glowing ever more brightly, the embers of a rare excitement. As always his wife had seen the future infinitely more clearly than had he. However, before those embers burst into all consuming flame, the subject needed much discussion and consideration.

He took his lovely wife by the hand and nodded towards the house. "Heather, I do think we need to go inside and discuss all this, don't you?" And without awaiting a reply, he led her towards Bray Barton's spacious kitchen.

Chapter Twenty

Despite George Tennant's innate caution and his need, always, to talk long and hard about and around a subject, he knew, standing that spring morning in the yard at Bray Barton, he would go along entirely with what Heather said. For her positive ideas, though partly hijacked by an enthusiasm even greater than that which habitually assailed her, were logical and soundly based. The long term future for them all at Bray Barton would be fraught; Holly Park was a first class farm and, at the right price, a good buy; and it was high time they owned the sod they turned.

So they agreed that if they could afford it, then they would purchase the holding. Out of courtesy and family loyalty, they broached the subject to Derek and Elaine. It proved to be a subject on which unanimity reigned. Indeed the outcome was so positive it virtually ensured that, unless something truly surprising ensued at the auction, then Holly Park would almost assuredly be theirs. For the younger couple had thought of the problems which could ensue in the future − indeed, almost certainly would with fresh generations coming along possibly wishing to farm Bray Barton. Thus Heather and George's desire to buy Holly Park was good news for them − the best. And Elaine, ever the sharper brained of the two, talked her husband into coming out with a quite generous offer to the Tennants within a couple of days of their being told of their Holly Park intentions. For Elaine could see that it was vital for her family's future at Bray Barton that she and Derek hold sole tenancy of the farm. That, in the short term, was not possible as they had insufficient capital. They did, however, have sufficient available to be able to make an offer for half of the Tennant's interest in the place − which, if accepted, would give them seventy-five per cent of the tenancy, with George and Heather retaining twenty-five per cent. The proposal made sense to all concerned and after mild wrangling – a wish for a slightly higher cash offer on the part of the Tennants, and the stipulation that the outgoing couple agree, in principle, that they would sell their remaining holding in Bray Barton at a price to be set by an independent valuer at a time when the Maunders had sufficient funds to complete the deal – the transaction was agreed. Thus a sizeable cheque was paid out by Derek and Elaine, using up most of their funds, Bray Barton became three quarters theirs, and the Tennants had sufficient capital to feel that Holly Park would soon be entirely their own.

And so it transpired. The auction was well attended – farmers always had an interest in seeing a farm sold, how much it fetched, who bought it. Few, however, actually desired Holly Park. Indeed, few wished to buy any land at all; the opposite, in fact. With farming the way it had become – income at best, static, overheads ever-rising, the majority would sell some, perhaps all, of their acres if the price was right. And Holly Park had notoriety of the kind which brought folk to witness its destiny, but dissuaded them from bidding for it. There were few farmhouses in Devon, after all, in which a murder had been committed. Strangely the knowledge that his daughter had been slain, and brutally, in Holly Park farmhouse did not in any way make George Tennant feel he did not wish to live in it. The opposite, in fact, for in a strange way, he felt he would be closer to her memory by living where she had lived – and died. Heather was a little more reticent in that sense, but any thoughts which intruded into her mind on that score were put aside quickly, classed as being squeamish and foolish – and the sole minus. To her there were so many plusses, and not least amongst them the fact that she, like her father, had always fancied owning, and farming, Holly Park.

Thus the farm was knocked down – for, probably, twenty per cent less than its true value even in such times of falling land prices – to Heather and George Tennant. Handling the financial side of things, as she did invariably, Heather signed a cheque to cover the deposit on the place, with the remainder due on the completion date, two months to the future.

And they were decidedly a hectic eight weeks, packing up at Bray Barton and using up copious amounts of money to buy implements and general dead stock for the farm. The buying of livestock they were going to delay until they had moved into the place, and knew exactly the amount of capital which remained in their account. "It's not going to be a great amount," mused Heather. "Even though we bought the farm at a very fair price, the money seems to have disappeared like snow before the sun – I'm not really sure what on – though machinery and implements are a fearsome price, of course. Still," she added in her customary confident tone, "there will be sufficient to buy in a reasonable basis, stock wise; we can build up over the years."

Thus amidst a welter of buying, planning and preparation did the days evaporate and it was a hot day in late July when George Tennant clambered aboard the old Land Rover to drive up the rocky lane towards the moor for probably the final time as joint working master of Bray Barton. The following morning Heather would take a cheque into their solicitors for the outstanding residue which had to be paid before the deeds of Holly Park were made over to them. She also had to sign various documents, he having signed his share as joint owner that very day in Tavistock, having had to go in to keep a dentist's appointment and having got the solicitor's somewhat reluctant agreement to his signing a day before, rather than having to go in again – "There are so many things I can be doing rather than use up part of another day going to Tavistock," he had opined.

"Most irregular," the solicitor had said with a sad shake of his head – but the Tennants were valued clients and such folk had to be looked after in this day and age, no matter how improper, technically, their requests.

The farmer started up the old four wheel drive and eased it across the yard waving a brief good-bye to young Robert as he went – a wave not returned. For young Robert stood at the kitchen door, a handkerchief held to his nose, looking most disgruntled with life. His grandfather had promised him a little earlier that he could go up to the moor in the Land Rover with him; unfortunately however, the lad had developed a bad nosebleed – something to which he tended to be prone – so Heather felt that he was best indoors, or at least, in the shade, away from the searing sun and the bumpy ride. There had been a paddy, but to no avail from the boy's point of view. Heather was a kind and loving woman but she was always firm when it came to children and once having made a decision, whether great or small, rarely changed it.

Thus it was George Tennant drove alone up the narrow track towards the moor, to perform a task which very occasionally came his way during a dry, hot spell. And this most certainly had been one of those – three weeks without rain, with temperatures as high as they had been for a decade or more. And the problem in such a period was water – or lack of it. With Bray Barton relying on the brook running down from the moor for so much of its water, the occasional efforts of children – or adults – building dams across the narrow bed of the stream up in the boulder strewn terrain above the farm, causing the diversion of the supply away from the farm and its parched stock, meant urgent action had to be taken. One look at the stream just after lunch had told the farmer that the amateur water engineers – or, possibly they were professional vandals – had been at it again. There had been a meagre – though adequate and constant – amount of water running down the previous day; now though, it was but the merest trickle – consequently seriously insufficient. Thus the tedious trip up onto the wild plateau to destroy the dam and return the water to its natural course – a similar journey to that which he had made with Arthur Maunder those many years before on the last day of that good man's life.

He steered the sturdy machine up the lane and onto the moor, then, revving up a little, angled it across a largish outcrop of rocks which hid a deep gully beside which ran the vital stream – at present, no doubt thanks to the help of young and mischievous hands, at a tangent which was diverting it well away from Bray Barton. He approached the outcrop and was about to slow and swing the Land Rover around so that it was parallel to the rocks when he found, suddenly, he was unable to move. He saw the rocks in front of him but his foot was, seemingly, frozen upon the accelerator, his arms locked with the wheel held in a tight grip – and he remembered no more. Darkness descended upon him as the Land Rover rattled on inexorably before crashing into the rocks, somersaulting over a lower outcrop of them to the side, then landing in the granite flanked gully.

George Tennant opened his eyes and gazed up at a face which he failed to recognise. "Good to see you with us at last, Mr Tennant," came the soft female voice. The woman seemed to George to have a massive crop of hair, and to be clad in white. His lips moved slowly and, it seemed to him, most painfully – and frustratingly, he was unable immediately to form his words.

The woman continued to gaze down at him but made no attempt to speak again; rather, she assumed an expression which suggested she expected him to try once more to talk. This he did – with a touch of success. "What happened?" he muttered, softly, slowly and painfully.

"We were rather hoping you would be able to tell us that," came the calm reply. "All we know is where you were found – in a gully up on Dartmoor with a wrecked Land Rover partially crushing you. How it happened only you can possibly know. You are, though, Mr Tennant, extremely fortunate to be alive. Indeed, when you were brought in your chances did not appear to be too promising. However, we were able to operate to stop the internal bleeding – which at the outset posed a major problem – then repair the very considerable internal damage which the accident brought about. The other injuries are a broken leg, which should cause no long-term problems, and a badly bruised head and face, including a broken nose and the loss of some teeth, which is why you find it both painful and difficult to talk at present. You have been unconscious for virtually three days. Now that you are awake and with us again, however, I feel we can probably say the worst is behind you."

"Heather," he muttered.

The doctor smiled. "Your wife has been here off and on throughout the time you have been with us. She went home about two hours ago to see that everything was all right there; the sister is phoning her now to inform her you have regained consciousness. She will be back in very soon I have no doubt."

She turned to go, then glanced back at her patient. "I see in your records, Mr Tennant, that you are an epileptic. Certainly in examining you when you were first admitted here there was strong evidence you had suffered a fit of some description and with your medical history, it was almost definitely epileptic. I assume you are taking medication for it?"

He nodded his head – painfully and slowly.

"Yet you still had a fit; have you had any others recently – in the past couple of years, for instance. Fits, black-outs – anything like that?"

He gazed up at her for several seconds, his entire body

immobile; then, again, he nodded his head.

"I thought so," replied the doctor. "We have picked up various things in the tests we have done on you to suggest you are not free from fits, though they probably vary considerably in strength. The one you had in your Land Rover, Mr Tennant, was a severe one. It was as well you were alone – and not driving on a public highway. It is unwise, to say the least, for you to continue to drive. Not that you will be in any fit state to do that for a while. But when you are ready to do so once more – you must not. In fact, you will not be allowed to. I shall have to report this to Swansea – for the sake of other road users, and for your own. Also, of course, it is the law as you probably know. I have informed your wife of this already – and she is in full agreement. In fact, I think she was relieved that real tragedy was not involved in all this. Apparently, your grandson was going to ride with you that afternoon, and would have done so if he had not been prevented by a nosebleed. Food for thought, Mr Tennant – is it not?"

The doctor's stare was unblinking – and not one which George Tennant could meet. Thus, he closed his eyes to avoid it. Her words, however, had hit their mark. He had been lashed, verbally, by this soft-voiced but intense woman; he felt deep guilt and an overwhelming sense of relief that Robert had not ridden with him that afternoon. He did not need anyone at Swansea to tell him to offer up his licence – he resolved, there and then, never to drive again until his accursed epilepsy had been neutralised permanently.

He closed his eyes and drifted off to sleep. When he awoke, Heather was sitting beside his bed, holding his right hand in hers. He smiled up at her wanly, whilst she bent forward and kissed him on the forehead.

His lips moved slowly, and ever painfully, but he knew exactly what he wished to articulate: "Sorry, Heather. I really am so sorry."

"There's nothing to be sorry about, darling. The main thing is you are going to get better, and come home to Holly Park. But no more driving George – you must promise me that."

He smiled as best he could, and nodded. "I promise," he whispered. He closed his eyes but then opened them again – promptly. "Holly Park – you mean you have signed the papers and the cheque?" he asked, his voice scarcely audible. In spite of his weakness, though, remembrance of their impending buying of, and moving into, their new home had returned to him suddenly.

"Despite all that has happened, Heather – in – in the past few days?" He paused to gather a little strength, then partially repeated himself; "Despite all that has, happened, you still finalised the deal over Holly Park?" His voice, though so very soft, still betrayed conflicting tones – of admiration over his wife's presence of mind and fortitude, of surprise she had proceeded at a time when obviously he was hovering on the brink of death and, possibly, mild chagrin that she could think of such practical matters when there was a distinct possibility she would be widowed that very same day.

As always, Heather Tennant was able to read her husband's mind and, thus, she answered his thoughts rather than his actual words. "Of course I finished the deal, George. Holly Park is now our home. The children and I will move in as soon as possible, and we will get the house comfortable and welcoming for when you are able to come out of hospital. As to running the farm, we will have to sort that out in a month or two. We shall most certainly need to take on somebody – a man with a feel for the land, as well as having had great experience at working on it. But there's no panic; fortunately we've no stock as yet, so we've a breathing space. And it's a breathing space we will be able to use to get you strong again – to return you to health. And time to allow the children to settle in; it could be that the place will have bad memories for little Robert; he will need a great deal of love and attention during the next few months. But it has no bad memories for me, George – only wonderful possibilities. My father fancied Holly Park, as I have said before, and I always have, ever since I was a young girl. And now it is ours; we own it, not rent it – we own it. I've worked the land – and earned my living from it – all my life, George, but this is the first time I have ever owned as much as a square yard. It's a wonderful feeling, darling – more wonderful than I can fully express. And it's made even more marvellous by the fact we will tread and work the land together – and our children, hopefully, will follow us, and theirs will follow them. That is what owning land is all about, George, the continuity of seed-time and harvest on soil that is yours –

along with triumphs and disasters – year in, year out, generation after generation. You do understand what I mean, George, do you not. I love you more than any words can ever say, and I hope we have so very many more years together. But land, darling, land which you nurture with your sweat and turn with your hands – that's everlasting, and more potent and powerful than any of us. You do understand George – please say you do."

Her husband gazed up at her for several seconds before he attempted to speak. Then he forced his mouth into a painful, crooked smile – and nodded slowly.

"I understand Heather, that being married to you is a privilege and joy beyond words – as well as being something of an adventure."

With that he gently squeezed her hand, closed his eyes, and fell into a contented sleep.